Waiting for Evening to Come

by

Glenn Berggoetz

Publisher's Note:

This is a work of fiction. All names, characters, places, and events are the work of the author's imagination.

Any resemblance to real persons, places, or events is coincidental.

Solstice Publishing - www.solsticepublishing.com

For my brother Lawrence – the best writer in the family.

Chapter One

In the summer of 1952 my family moved from Churubusco, Indiana, to the outskirts of Huntington, Indiana. It wasn't much of a change for a ten year old.

Our move was from one farm house to another. Dad worked for the railroad, and even though he wasn't a farmer, he always insisted on living out in the country. We always had a large garden, mostly tended to by Mom. I liked it this way. Having grown up in a rural setting, the thought of living in a house in a town, even one of only five hundred people, wasn't very enticing to me.

Our new home was a pretty typical white, two-story farm house. On the inside, it was rather stark with all white walls. We had a barn out back, as well as a large shed, and out beyond the corn fields were some forests. What I was most excited about, though, was the huge reservoir I heard about that wasn't too far away. I pictured myself spending long summer days swimming and exploring there, dropping a pole in the water, and staring at the floating red plastic ball for hours on end as the clouds floated by – I was sure our new home was going to be a little bit of heaven.

I helped Mom and Dad unload the pickup truck, carrying small boxes up the two wooden steps and in through the back door to the huge kitchen, sometimes taking them into the living room or even up the stairs to one of the bedrooms. Mom and Dad handled the larger ones. Dad and a couple of his buddies had already brought over the furniture earlier that morning. We worked silently for the most part. About all that was said was an occasional "Here, take this" from Dad to me or a "Can you get me a glass of water?" from him to Mom.

Before long, it was just me and my tall, slender father carrying boxes in as Mom began to empty out some of them in the kitchen, taking out plates and bowls and pots and putting them away in the cupboards and cabinets, her long brown hair pulled back in a ponytail.

We worked this way for a while, the boxes and items in the back of the truck slowly dwindling. Eventually Dad walked into the kitchen and announced, "This is the last one."

Mom gave the smallest of smiles as he moved past her. He placed the box with a few others along the wall. I stood in the corner, idly looking through a box of kitchen utensils.

"How're things comin' along in here?" he asked.

"Pretty good, I guess," said Mom. "Still a lot to do, though."

Dad took a seat at the kitchen table and looked around the room.

"We're gonna like it here, Mary," he said.

"I'm sure we will."

"I still can't believe the price we got on this place," said Dad. "It's almost as if they were givin' it away."

"It sat empty for quite a while."

"Knowing what we now know about the neighborhood, I can understand why," he said.

Dad looked over at me.

"What're ya doin', Jack?"

"Nothing, sir."

"Why don't you go upstairs and put your things away," Mom said. "I'll get us some lunch together. When you're done, you can have a sandwich."

"Yes, ma'am." I went up to my room.

My bedroom was pretty big. It had two windows – one looked out to the back over the fields and towards the forests, the other to the west, over more fields. Far off in the distance, I noticed another farm house. It was too far away to see if anything was going on there. I wondered if there might be someone there my age I might become friends with.

It only took me maybe fifteen minutes to get all my things unpacked and put away. My clothes fit neatly into the dresser, and my few toys looked pretty good on the shelf in the closet.

I went downstairs to find that Mom had placed a sandwich and a glass of water on the table for me. Dad was already eating his food. I sat down and began to munch on my food.

"Are all your things put away?" asked Dad.

"Yes, sir."

"Good."

I ate in silence, chewing quickly – I hadn't realized how hungry I had become. He noticed.

"Worked up quite an appetite, huh?"

"Yes, sir," I answered.

"Make sure you chew your food, Jack," said Mom.

"I will."

Dad and I finished off our sandwiches as Mom put some glasses and cups in a cupboard.

"What can I help with now?" I asked.

Mom looked at Dad.

"Can you use his help out in the barn?" she asked.

"He'll just get in the way," he said and looked at me. "Why don't you take your bike and head on down to the reservoir?"

I quickly grew excited.

"How far away is it?"

"Just about a mile down the road there," said Dad as he pointed to the west. "From what the real estate guy told me."

"Okay."

I bounded off the chair and went to the back door.

"Make sure you're back in time for supper," said Mom.

"Yes, ma'am," I called out over my shoulder as I burst out of the house, the screen door slamming behind me.

"Don't slam the door!" Dad yelled.

I flinched but kept running to the barn to gather my bike. It was sunny and hot, so the water would be warm and comfortable to wade in. I couldn't wait to experience the reservoir – the only bodies of water I had been around before had been some small lakes near Churubusco that really weren't much more than big ponds.

I got on my bike, pedaled down our long, dirt driveway, and onto the dirt road that would take me to the reservoir. A minute or so after setting out, I stopped and looked back toward the house to see how far I'd gone. Our new home was still in clear view since the corn was no more than knee high. What I found fascinating was the huge dust cloud I'd kicked up from my bike in my haste to get to the reservoir. It hung over the road, drifting listlessly over the corn. I couldn't believe my little bike and I had created such a huge cloud.

After staring at the swirling dust for a long moment, I took off again, this time pedaling even more furiously than before to see if I could stir up an even bigger cloud. Thirty seconds later I stopped and turned around. Breathing hard, I was enthralled with what I'd done. I watched the cloud drift over the corn, some of the heavier pieces of dirt settling while the smaller particles lazed about in the air. A grin crept over my face.

I hopped back onto the seat of the bike and took off again, determined to ride faster and longer than before, to stir up the biggest dust cloud any ten-year-old boy had ever kicked up.

I put my head down and pedaled as hard as I could. I rode my bike so hard that before I knew it I saw a bead of sweat drip off the tip of my nose and onto the handlebars.

When my energy waned a bit, I slammed on my brakes and came to an abrupt stop, kicking up as much dust as I could. I looked back at my work – the dust cloud had grown to what seemed like epic proportions to my young mind.

For at least a minute, I simply stood astride my bike and watched the veil of dirt particles drift, amazed that I could produce such a spectacle. When my breath came back to me, I resumed my position on my bike and took off again.

I pedaled and pedaled, doing everything I could to surpass my previous efforts. My head was down, aerodynamic, cutting the resistance as much as I could as I sped along the deserted dirt road. With sweat dripping from my face, I slammed on the brakes and turned to see what I had created.

The cloud was as impressive as the last one, but not better. Still, I couldn't help but smile as I stared at it. I had created something bigger than I could ever have imagined possible.

"That's quite a cloud you've stirred up there."

I snapped my head around. In my cloud-making fury I hadn't realized that I had reached the house that I had seen from my bedroom window a little while earlier.

I stood astride my bike and stared, the smile on my face having dashed away. There, sitting on a big, wooden rocking chair on the porch of the house that was only about sixty feet back off the road, was an old man. An old brown man. There was a smile on his face and a bottle of soda in his hand.

It was only later that I would realize there was more than an old brown man in my range of vision. The brick farm house was definitely older than our place – probably built in the 1800s – but it was in immaculate shape. The yard was flush with flowers and carefully-trimmed bushes. Two large oak trees framed the area and kept most of it in the shade. So entranced was I by the strange creature who was speaking to me that none of these things registered in my mind until later.

"Why don't you come on up here and sit a while," said the man.

Mesmerized, I swung my right leg over the bike and walked it up to the old man's yard. I moved tentatively. When I reached the yard, I laid my bike on the ground and continued up to where the old brown man sat and slowly rocked in his chair. It felt like it took me fifteen minutes to cross the grass and reach the porch. When I did, the man motioned to a rocking chair that sat motionless a couple feet from the one he was in with a small wooden table between the chairs.

"Have a seat."

Slowly, I did as told. He took a drink from his bottle of soda.

"There's only one thing beats a cold drink on a hot day, and that's a hot woman on a cold night." The man smiled mischievously. "But not by much," he added.

He winked at me and handed me the bottle. Hesitatingly, I took the soda. The old brown man nodded at me.

"Go ahead, have a drink," said the man. "You have to have worked up quite a thirst with all that bike ridin' you've been doin'."

Slowly, I took a sip, not even tasting the soda, and handed the bottle back to the man. For a long moment I sat still as he looked out over the corn fields and rocked contentedly.

"I could spend the rest of my life right here, just listenin' to the corn stalks whisperin' to each other and the birds singin'. Couldn't you?" He glanced at me with a smile.

Eventually, I replied with a small nod. The man took another drink from the bottle of soda and passed it back to me. I took another small drink and gave the bottle back. The man placed the bottle on the table between us. He picked up a pocketknife and a small piece of wood from the table. He leisurely carved on the wood, content with the silence. I watched his hands as he worked – large, brown, adept hands that skillfully manipulated the knife and the wood. We both sat silently for a long minute.

"You move into the old Sullivan place up the road there?" he asked.

I nodded.

"It looks like we're neighbors," the man said. "Do you have any brothers?"

I shook my head.

"Sisters?"

I shook my head again.

"So it's just you and your folks?"

I nodded.

"Well, I bet you and your parents are gonna like it here. It's a beautiful place to live."

He smiled playfully, and we resumed our quiet sitting as he went casually back and forth from carving on the wood to looking out over the fields.

"Is your daddy gonna take over farming the land?"

Hesitatingly, I said, "No. He works for the railroad."

"Does he now? I spent forty-three years myself workin' for the railroad. Got to meet a lotta good people."

The silence descended again. The man sometimes looked out over the fields and sometimes carved on the wood. I mostly looked out over the fields. When I could, I stole a glance at his peculiar hands or face. After a little while the man spoke again.

"It's about that time that I head on in for my afternoon nap. It sure was nice meetin' you. Feel free to finish off that soda if you'd like."

He winked at me, placed the pocketknife and the wood, which was starting to take the form of a tiny squirrel, on the little table between the chairs, and walked in through the front door of the house.

I remained in the rocking chair, confused. Was this man sick? He acted as if he was healthy, but his skin was unlike anything I had ever seen before. I had heard of something called the Big C that was awful to have – did this man have the Big C? And if he did, could I get it from having taken a drink out of the same bottle he'd taken a drink from?

Ten minutes later, I was still slowly rocking in the chair and no closer to understanding what was going on with this man. I finally got up, went to my bike, and pedaled off in the direction of the reservoir.

When I reached my destination, I found it to be almost unbelievably large. I could barely make out the trees on the other side, they were so far away. At ten years old, the reservoir seemed like an ocean to me. I should have been overwhelmed, awed by the sight, but my mind couldn't stop thinking about the old brown man. Was he maybe so old – older than anyone I had ever seen before – that his skin had changed color? Would that happen to me if I lived long enough? To Mom and Dad? Grandpa and Grandma seemed really old, but their skin was the same color as mine. Maybe this man had some bizarre disease I had never heard of, maybe some disease they only have in the jungles of the Amazon, but I wondered how he would contract some Amazonian disease when he was living in Indiana.

I parked my bike against a tree and explored the paths that ran through the woods. I saw plenty of squirrels and rabbits, and even a small garter snake, but none of this excited me as it normally would have, so fixated was I with the old man. After a couple hours of wandering and wondering, I made my way back to my bike and rode home.

When I pedaled past the old brown man's house, I slowed down a little and looked up onto the porch, but he wasn't there. I continued on home. When I arrived, I parked my bike in the barn and entered the house through the back door, making sure not to slam the screen door like I had earlier. Mom was just starting to put dinner on the table.

"I was starting to wonder where you were," said Mom.

The kitchen was already in order. I could see through the doorway leading into the living room that that room was also in good shape. I sat down at the table.

"Did you have fun?" Mom asked.

"Yes, ma'am."

"You hungry?"

"Yes'm."

Dad entered the kitchen.

"Somethin' smells good."

"Take a seat, and I'll get your plate ready," said Mom.

Dad sat down at the table next to me.

"How was the reservoir?" Dad asked me.

"It was neat. I liked it."

"What'd ya do there?" Mom asked.

"Nothing much," I answered. "Just walked around and explored a bit. I waded around in the water some. I saw a snake."

"Wow," said Mom. "Was it a big one?"

"Not really," I answered. "Just a little garter snake."

"Were there many other people there?" she asked.

"No. I did see a couple picnic tables, though, so people must go there sometimes."

"Maybe on the weekends it gets busy," Mom said.

"Maybe," I said.

She placed plates of food in front of me and Dad, then brought over a plate for herself and sat down. We all bowed our heads and folded our hands. Dad prayed.

"We humbly come before you, Jesus, to thank you for this food, for this family, and for our new home. Please continue to bless us and keep us. We pray this in Your name. Amen."

"Amen," echoed Mom.

We ate silently for a full minute.

"I met a man," I said. "I think he might be sick."

"Did you meet 'im at the reservoir?" asked Mom.

"No, he lives in that house down the road a ways on the way to the reservoir. He looked really funny."

Anger flushed my father's face.

"You mean you met that nigger I heard about?"

"No, you always say niggers're black," I said. "This man was brown, not black."

"What do you think a nigger is?" Dad said. "Anyone from light brown to pitch black is a nigger. I don't want you to have anything to do with him. Ya hear me?"

"Yes, sir."

"All niggers is trouble," said Dad.

"He seemed nice," I said.

He shook his head in disgust. Mom remained quiet.

"That was just so he could take advantage of you later," he said. "Why, he'll try to get all nice and cozy with you, and then one day he'll find out you got a dollar in your pocket, and he'll trick you right out of it. Steal it right out from under your nose. That's all niggers is. They're just a bunch of lazy, no-good thieves. You can't trust 'em for one second. If I find out you've been hangin' around that nigger down the road, or any nigger for that matter, I'll give ya a lickin' you won't soon forget. Ya hear me, boy?"

"Yes, sir."

"Your father's right, Jack." Mom said. "You need to be careful around people like that. At your age, the best thing to do is just avoid 'em."

"But why is his skin brown?" I asked.

"Because God cursed niggers," said Dad. "Thousands of years ago when Cain murdered Abel, God banished Cain from his people, and to make sure his people never took him back, God put a mark on Cain that all people would immediately recognize and that would let them know they shouldn't associate with him. The mark God put on Cain was to turn him into a nigger. Niggers are a cursed people, and don't you forget it. Now I don't wanna hear any more about it. Eat yer food."

We finished the meal in silence.

The next morning, before the sun got too hot, I got my bike out of the barn and headed off for the reservoir.

I didn't stir up the dust like I had the day before. In fact, on this morning I went extra slow, doing my best to make sure I stirred up as little dust as possible so I wouldn't draw attention to myself.

As I neared the old man's house, I stopped to check to see if I had stirred up a dust cloud. I had, but it wasn't nearly as big as the ones from the day before. After a moment, I turned my attention to the house. I stared up at the porch, but the man wasn't there. I noticed something moving near the side of the house – he was tending to some flowers.

I debated what to do. Should I turn back? That didn't seem like a very good option. I really wanted to explore the reservoir again, this time with a clear head that wasn't clouded with thoughts of the old man and whether he was sick or why his skin was a different color from mine. But if I continued on, I didn't want to have this man trick me up onto his porch again and have him hurt me in some way. After a long moment, my desire to explore the reservoir won out.

I readied myself on my bike, taking off at top speed, my head down, my legs churning. A few seconds later I was in front of the man's house.

"Good morning!"

I turned my head just a little and looked out of the corner of my eye to see the old man standing and waving to me. There was a huge smile on his face. It seemed genuine, as best as I could tell. I quickly remembered my parents' words, refocused my eyes on the ground that was rushing by below me, and pedaled on.

Thirty seconds later, I slowed to a more normal speed and looked back toward the old man's house. He was back tending to his flowers. I released a deep breath of relief. Soon, I would be exploring the reservoir.

When I returned home a few hours later for lunch, the old man wasn't on his porch or out in his yard. I was glad.

After lunch, Mom sent me up to my room for a while. I had been playing with my Lincoln Logs for a bit when I stood up from the floor to stretch. I looked out my window and saw a figure walking down the road toward our house. I moved closer to get a better look. A moment later I could see that it was the old man walking our way, carrying something. I stared. A minute later I could see he had a picnic basket.

I continued to stare at him. He walked slowly, but his movements were smooth and graceful. Most of the time, his head faced up as he looked at the sky. As he drew nearer, I could see there was a look of wonder and joy on his face. I stood in the window, paralyzed, staring at this strange creature.

Before I knew it, the old man had turned into our driveway and was walking toward our back door. I snapped out of my paralysis, moved quietly to the stairwell, and tiptoed down the stairs. When I reached the bottom, I stepped softly across the living room until I came to the doorway that led into the kitchen. I peeked around the corner to see Mom at the sink, drying some dishes as she stared out the window. A moment later, a frown crossed her face. She shook her head as she put down the glass she was drying and placed the towel on the counter. She moved to the back door as a few gentle knocks filled the room.

I peeked a tiny bit farther around the corner to see the old man standing on the wooden steps outside the back door. The picnic basket was still in his hand. He had a joyful smile on his face. Mom reached the door.

"Can I help you?" she asked, her voice flat.

"Hello, ma'am," said the old man. "My name is Benjamin Rhodes – I'm your neighbor just the down the road a bit."

"Good to meet you," she said curtly.

"I just wanted to introduce myself and bring you a little welcome gift," said Benjamin.

He put the picnic basket down and carefully took a pie out of it. He presented it to Mom. She opened the screen door just enough for him to hand her the pie.

"It's peach," he said.

"That's very nice of you." Mom spoke formally.

She took the pie from the smiling Benjamin and allowed the screen door to close back up.

"Are you all getting settled in all right?" he asked.

"We have most everything put away by now," Mom said, her voice still toneless.

"That's good," he said. "Moving can be awful stressful. It's always nice to get it done and over with."

"I imagine you're right on that account."

His face lit up a little bit as he noticed me peeking around the corner. He moved his head a couple inches so he could see me a little better and winked. I could see Mom turning in an attempt to catch a look at what had caught his attention. I jerked my head back and out of view.

"Well," said Benjamin. "If I can ever be of any help to you or your family in any way, or if you ever need to borrow anything, or if your husband needs help moving anything or can't seem to find a tool he needs, you feel free to call on me and I'll help out in any way I can."

"Okay."

"You have a good day now, ma'am"

"I'll try," answered my mother.

I peeked back around the corner to see Benjamin, still smiling, pick up the picnic basket and walk off. Mom carried the pie to the window by the sink and watched him go. After waiting until he was down the driveway and back out on the road, she moved to the trash can and dropped the pie in it. She went back to her dishes and picked up her towel. I waited for a moment before entering the kitchen.

"You're supposed to be up in your room," Mom said without looking at me.

"Yes, ma'am."

I watched her work for a while.

"Why did you throw the pie away?"

"We don't eat no food prepared by no niggers."

Mom never looked at me. I stood in silence as she thoroughly dried a plate.

"Go on back up to your room." She still didn't look at me. I did as told.

I began the next day early by spending a couple hours exploring the woods behind the corn field and seeing all the neat things that were back there. There was a small creek that at one point people had used for dumping items they no longer needed. I came across an old ice box, a rusty washing machine, a bunch of old tires, and, best of all, an old rusted out car that had to be more than thirty years old. I couldn't believe my luck. The car had a backseat that was in pretty good shape for the most part. I imagined I was

John Dillinger, and I was on the lam from the cops. This car was the place I would go to hide out and get some sleep with my stash of money safely hidden in the old ice box.

After thoroughly investigating all of my new finds, I decided to head to the reservoir and made it there without seeing Benjamin. I had a great time swimming and splashing around in the water, chasing after a couple frogs, and hiking through the woods that seemed to go on forever. Eventually I got hungry and decided to make my way home for some lunch. As I was riding my bike in that direction and neared Benjamin's house, I could see he was on his porch. He was rocking slowly as he carved on a piece of wood. There was a big pitcher of lemonade on the table.

As I had done the day before, I put my head down and pedaled hard to get past Benjamin's place. As I flew by the house, he hollered out, "Hello there!" I pretended I hadn't heard him and kept pedaling.

When I rode up the driveway, Mom was hanging wet clothes up on the clothesline. She called out, "Did you have a good swim?"

I rode up to her. "Yes, ma'am."

"What else did you do there? Did you see any more snakes?"

"Just a couple little garter snakes – I haven't seen any big ones yet. And I found a stretch of woods I hadn't seen before, so I explored around in it for a while. There was an old campsite back in there with a bunch of old burned and rusted-out tin cans. I bet there were hoboes living there."

"Wow, sounds exciting," she said.

"It was pretty neat," I said. "I really like it here. Do you like it here?"

"Yeah, it's nice," said Mom. "It's not perfect, but we could do much worse."

She hung a shirt on the line.

"Did you see that nigger when you rode by his place?" she asked.

"No. I kept my head down when I went by his house."

"That's good. We're just lookin' out for you, ya know."

"I know."

"Why don't you put your bike away and get cleaned up. Your father'll be home soon. We'll eat as soon as he gets in."

"Okay," I said.

I smiled meekly and walked off with my bike. I stopped after a few steps and looked back at her.

"Hey, Ma?"

"Yes?"

I thought for a long moment.

"Never mind," I said and walked my bike up into the barn.

***

That weekend, Dad took me into town for the first time. He wanted me to get a haircut. Afterward, we were going to stop at a hardware store to pick up some things.

The barber was nice. He and Dad talked a bit while I sat stone still in the chair, my eyes looking straight ahead, afraid that even the littlest shifting about might move my head a tiny bit and mess up the crew cut I was receiving.

I thought about how a few years earlier I used to cry when I got a haircut. Not loud, sobbing cries, but quiet whimpers followed by a tear or two trickling down my cheek. I wondered why I had done that. The haircut hadn't hurt in any way. Did I think I was Samson and would lose all my power by having my hair cut? I had no idea why I used to cry during haircuts. I just remembered that one time when I was six years old I felt no desire to cry while having my hair trimmed. It was perplexing.

The conversation between my father and the barber faded into the background while I continued to think. I noticed that as Dad and I drove into town, Huntington had seemed much bigger than Churubusco – there were even a couple traffic lights we passed through. It was a little scary. I wondered how big my school would be. Would my teacher be nice? Would I make friends quickly? Would the kids at school play baseball? Would they be Cubs fans, or would they like the Reds? Or worse, would they like the dreaded Cardinals?

The next thing I knew my haircut was done. The barber commended me for being such a good customer. I thanked him as I had been taught to do. A minute later Dad and I were walking down the street to the hardware store. Along the way, we stopped into a soda fountain. He bought me an ice cream cone, which made me really happy as I rarely got such treats. We resumed our walk, me licking on the ice cream cone as we went along.

"How is it? Is it good?" Dad asked.

"Yes, sir."

"So how are you liking the new house?"

"I like it," I said.

"Is your bedroom okay?"

"Mm hmm."

"Good," said Dad. "You got enough room to play?"

"Yes, sir," I said. He smiled. "I really like the reservoir, and the woods back behind the fields are fun, too. Did you know there's an old rusted out car back there?"

"No, I didn't know that," Dad answered with a little laugh.

"It's really neat. The back seat isn't in too bad of shape. There's also an old ice box and some tires."

"Interesting."

"Do you think there's any chance any bank robbers may have hidden out back there at some point after robbing a bank?" I asked.

"I guess there's always that chance," Dad said.

I smiled at that thought.

"You'll just have to be careful when the corn gets taller than you do – it can be pretty easy to get lost in a cornfield when the stalks get tall," Dad said. "Just remember that the sun always comes up to the east and sets in the west. Our house is on the north edge of the corn field where you found all that stuff. Can you remember that?"

"Yes, sir."

We walked along. I looked all about as I continued licking on the ice cream cone. I had never seen so many stores and cars and people in my life, other than on the occasional drive into Fort Wayne. A minute later, we reached the hardware store.

"Here we are," said Dad. "Just the place we've been lookin' for."

He opened the door, and we walked in. We stood inside the door for a moment as he looked around and as I kept working on my ice cream cone.

"I think what I need is in the back," said Dad. "Go ahead and look around a little, but don't get in any trouble. And be careful with your ice cream. I'll be back in a few minutes."

He walked off to the back of the store. I stood still for a moment, licking the ice cream cone and scanning everything in sight. I tentatively moved around the store. I walked down the first aisle, looking casually at the unfamiliar items on the shelves, making sure not to touch any of them, paying more attention to my ice cream than to what I saw.

I reached the end of the aisle and started to turn the corner when I suddenly came face-to-face with Benjamin. He held a number of items in his hands. A big smile appeared on his face.

"Well, hey there, young man," said Benjamin. "Out pickin' up a few things?"

I froze. A moment later, I glanced to the back corner of the store where Dad had walked to, but all I could see were tall shelves and a display. I looked up, and there was Benjamin smiling down at me. I quickly turned my attention back to my ice cream cone.

"I'm just gettin' a few things myself," he said. "There's always somethin' that needs to be done around the place."

He looked at the ice cream cone in my hands.

"That looks like a mighty tasty ice cream cone you have there. Is it good?"

I nodded, wondering if he would try to steal it from me.

"And I see you got yourself a haircut," said Benjamin. "It looks very nice."

I said nothing. The smile never left his face.

"You're gonna have to stop on by again someday and tell me all about yourself," said Benjamin. "All right?"

I nodded, knowing that that would never happen. I shouldn't lie, but I was afraid – afraid of what my father would do should he see me talking to him, and afraid of what Benjamin, a nigger, might do to me.

"All right then," he said. "You have a good day now."

He moved along down the aisle. I peeked around the corner and watched him walk away. Benjamin turned the corner at the end of the aisle and disappeared from sight.

I stood motionless, staring at the place where I last saw him. A shadow fell across me, and I jumped. I looked up to see Dad standing over me, a couple small items in his hand.

"You see anything you like?" he asked.

I shook my head.

"You don't need any toggle bolts or anything?"

"No, sir."

He smiled and put his arm around my shoulder.

"Come on then," said Dad. We walked up to pay for the items he had.

That Monday morning I got my bike out of the barn and rode to the reservoir. I meandered at first, making sure to keep from stirring up too much dust. As I approached Benjamin's house, I pedaled fast.

As I passed his place, I glanced over to see him in the yard and waving at me. I put my head back down and rode on. Not fifty feet past his yard, though, a sharp rock flattened my front tire.

I got off my bike and stood with my back toward his house as I looked at the tire and tried to think of what I should do. I looked back down the road toward my house, and then in the other direction toward the reservoir. Should I wheel the bike back home? Should I maybe just leave it on the side of the road and walk the rest of the way to the reservoir, then take the bike back to the house when I was done playing?

"Got a flat there?"

Before I knew it, Benjamin was but twenty feet away and walking toward me. For a few moments I was motionless, then I nodded in response to his question.

"Let's wheel her on up to the shed and see if we can't get her patched up for ya," said Benjamin.

He took hold of the handlebars and wheeled my bike up his driveway. I followed a few steps behind him. The dirt driveway went past the house and curved around behind it. Just like with our place, there was a barn and a shed in back. The yard behind his house was every bit as immaculate as the yard in the front with flowers everywhere, a vegetable garden off to the side, and a big shade tree protecting much of the yard.

He stopped and took a deep breath.

"Smell that?"

"Smell what?"

"The smell of rain is in the air," said Benjamin. "Don't you smell it?"

I sniffed a couple times.

"No."

"You make a note in your head about what the air smells like today," he said. "Compare it to the next nice day we have. You'll notice there'll be a little tingle missin' from the air on that nice day."

"But there aren't hardly any clouds in the sky," I said.

"Just you wait a couple hours," said Benjamin. "You'll see these rows of corn around us dancin' with delight over the drink they're gettin'. Why, it's probably a good thing you got this flat tire, 'cause if you didn't it's liable you'd've got caught in the storm while you were down at the reservoir and soaked yourself through an' through."

He resumed wheeling the bike toward his place. We reached the shed a few moments later, and Benjamin parked the bicycle by the door.

"I'll be right back," he said.

Benjamin ducked into the shed. I didn't know what to do. For a moment, I considered simply turning and running home and letting him steal my bike like it appeared he was trying to do. I stared back toward my house, wondering if I could make it out of his yard and out onto the road before he noticed me running off. Before I could decide, he emerged from the shed. He carried some tools and patching materials.

"If I've patched one tire, I've patched a hundred." He went to the bike and deftly began to work on the tire, his hands moving smoothly, gracefully.

"We'll just get that tire off, pop the inner tube out, find that hole, and get her fixed up in no time."

Like a flash, Benjamin had the wheel off the bike and was removing the tire from the rim.

"We'll just get that tire off like this," he said as he let me see what he was doing. I was amazed at how quickly he worked.

He got the tire off the rim and removed the inner tube, letting me see everything he was doing. He gave the inner tube a good looking over.

"There she is."

He showed me the puncture.

"This shouldn't be too hard," said Benjamin.

He cut off a patch from the material he had and glued it onto the inner tube. I watched closely. Over the next few minutes, he put the tube back into the tire, and slid it back on the rim. He worked quietly, efficiently.

"I'll let you screw that wheel back onto the bike," said Benjamin. "I'll go get the pump."

I nodded, grabbed the pliers, and reattached the wheel to the bike while he ducked back into the shed. Benjamin reappeared a moment later with a tire pump.

"Looks like we're in business." He held up the tire pump and looked down at me. "Hey, you're doin' some good work there."

A small smile creased my face. Benjamin pulled a red handkerchief out of his back pocket and wiped some sweat from his forehead as I finished putting the wheel back on the bike, double checking to make sure the bolt was tight.

"We better let that tire set for a few minutes before we pump her up so that glue has a chance to do her job," said Benjamin. "Can I interest you in some lemonade?"

I hesitated. We weren't supposed to eat any food prepared by niggers, but lemonade wasn't food. Maybe it would be okay. I was thirsty.

"It's nice and cold," he added.

I felt another little smile appear on my face.

"Okay," I said.

A huge grin broke out on his face.

"All right then." He motioned to a couple lawn chairs with a small table between them under the huge shade tree not far from the barn. "Why don't you make yourself comfortable there. I'll be right back with a couple cold lemonades."

I nodded and moved to the chairs as he went up to the back of the house.

I sat down and looked around at the flowers, the vegetable garden, the clothesline, and the well-tended grass. All around, the yard was surrounded by corn. Everything was comforting. The smile on my face grew.

A moment later, Benjamin emerged from the house with two glasses of lemonade. He reached me a few moments later and handed me one of the drinks.

"Here ya go."

"Thank you," I said.

He sat down in the chair next to me.

"Do you realize we don't even know each other's names? Mine's Benjamin."

"I knew your name – I heard it when you brought the pie to our house," I said.

"Did you now?"

I nodded.

"Did you like the pie?"

My heart sank. I knew with him being a nigger that we weren't supposed to eat any food he'd made, but I also knew he was a person, and it wasn't his fault that Cain killed Abel. If I had made him something to eat, had spent an hour or two of my time trying to do something nice for him only to have him throw the food away, I'd be awfully sad. There was only one thing I could say.

"Yeah, it was good."

"I'm glad you liked it. What's your name?" he asked.

"I'm Jack."

"That's a fine name." He smiled and nodded. We sat quietly for a few moments, sipping our lemonades. I felt myself suddenly become a little nervous. Benjamin seemed completely at ease.

"How do you like your new house?" he asked.

"I like it all right."

"How 'bout your folks? Do they like it too?"

"I think so."

We both sat quietly for a little while. Eventually, tentatively, I decided to find out more about him.

"Do you live here by yourself?" I asked.

"For the last six years I have. Ever since my Addie died."

"Was she your wife?"

Benjamin smiled.

"Yep. And my girlfriend."

We sat quietly again for a short while and sipped on our lemonades. A little more confidently, I asked another question.

"Do you have any kids?"

Benjamin smiled again, this time wistfully.

"Had one."

He took a long sip of his drink.

"He was killed in World War II," he finally said. "He was a fine boy."

We sipped silently on our lemonades for a while, looking out over the fields.

"Where'd you move here from?" Benjamin asked.

"Churubusco."

"How'd you like it there?"

"It was okay," I said. "A lot like here. No reservoir, though."

"You really like that reservoir, don't you?"

"Yeah."

"I bet you're a good swimmer."

I nodded. Benjamin smiled. Slowly, I smiled too. We resumed sitting quietly. I finished my lemonade.

"Can I get you another glass?" he asked.

"No thank you."

"Let's go check on that tire of yours and make sure we can get her pumped up okay and get ya home before the rains come."

We put our glasses on the small table between us and walked over to the bike. Benjamin took a deep breath.

"Can you smell the rain yet?" he asked.

I took a deep breath.

"I think so," I said.

He grinned.

We reached the bike. He pumped up the tire.

"This'll only take a minute," he said.

Benjamin worked hard putting air into the tire.

"It looks like it's holding so far," he said.

He finished filling the tire with air.

"Now let's see here," he said.

Benjamin bounced the bike on its front tire a few times.

"Seems okay. Why don't you hop on it there?"

I swung my leg up and over and sat on the bike.

"It looks like it's holdin' up just fine," he said. "I think you'll be all right."

"Thank you for your help," I said. "And thanks for the lemonade."

"You're quite welcome, Jack" replied Benjamin. "You feel free ta stop on by anytime you want to, okay?"

I couldn't help but smile a little bit.

"Okay," I said.

I pedaled down the driveway and turned toward my house. As I turned, I looked back to see Benjamin waving goodbye to me – I waved back. I rode along languidly and thought about things. I was happy but strangely confused. He seemed so nice, and his smile couldn't help but make me smile as well. I noticed something else when I was with him – I felt unusually calm. While I was nervous at first, before long I noticed that being in his presence felt like being wrapped up in my favorite blanket on a cold winter night with a cup of hot cocoa nestled in my hands. But Mom and Dad were both so adamant that Benjamin was a bad person and that I needed to stay away from him. Could they be wrong? Maybe they weren't wrong, simply mistaken.

These thoughts tossed about in my head for the next few minutes. By the time I turned my bike into our driveway, I had reached the conclusion that my parents were mistaken, and my happiness returned. As I pedaled up the driveway I went by the kitchen window, where I saw Mom at work at the sink. I waved happily to her, and she waved back, a rare smile on her face.

After parking my bike in the barn, I went up to the house and entered the kitchen. There was a bit of a confused look on her face.

"Why are you home so early?" she asked.

"I didn't want to get caught in the rain while down at the reservoir," I answered.

"What?"

Mom looked out the window and stared at the sunshine.

"What makes you think it's gonna rain?" she asked.

"I can smell it coming," I said.

A bemused look appeared on her face.

"I'll be playing in my room," I said, scampering upstairs.

That evening Mom and Dad and I gathered in the living room after dinner. He handed me the comics page from the newspaper. I spread it out on the floor and laid on my stomach to read them. Dad read another section of the paper while she sewed up one of his shirts.

Outside, it was raining steadily. It had been raining for hours. Dad put down his paper and listened for a few moments.

"That sure is a nice rain," Dad said. "Cool things down a bit."

"It is nice," Mom said. "It'll be good sleeping weather tonight."

"It sure will," he replied.

They went quiet. I read *Beetle Bailey*.

"What'd you do today, Jack?" he asked.

I hesitated for just a moment before saying, "I went down to the reservoir again."

"Did you get rained on?"

"No," I said. "I only stayed there a little while before coming home. I could smell the rain comin'."

"You could smell the rain comin'?" Dad asked.

"Yeah. There was a little tingle in the air," I said.

Mom and Dad looked at each other and smiled.

"I guess our boy's growin' up," she said.

"I reckon he is," he said.

They looked at me. I smiled and went back to reading the comics.

"Hey," Dad said as he turned his attention to Mom. "One of the guys at the rail yard said we should come to his church this weekend."

"It's not a Catholic church, is it?" Mom asked.

"No, it's Protestant. He said the people there are really nice. They have a great pastor who delivers good sermons. It's over in Mt. Etna."

"That's not too far from here, is it?"

"No, not too terribly far," Dad said.

"We'll have to give it a try," Mom said.

"All right. I'll get the directions from 'im tomorrow. We'll go on Sunday."

I looked up to see Mom smile her assent before going back to her sewing. Dad returned his attention to the paper.

A mild sense of dread came over me – there went my Sunday morning. I didn't like church much in the summer. When school was in session, it was even worse because having to go on Sundays made it feel like I only had one day off a week, which made me really hate it. I silently hoped Mom and Dad would find something to dislike about the church or the pastor.

The next morning I decided I better walk to the reservoir. The roads were exceedingly muddy, and I didn't have fenders on my bike. Riding over there would leave me with mud all over the back of my shirt and quite a bit on my face as well.

As I approached Benjamin's house I could faintly hear a wonderful, melodic voice singing the old standard "Down in the Valley." The words drifted faintly to me.

"Down in the valley

"Valley so low

"Hang your head over

"Hear the wind blow

"Hear the wind blow, love

"Hear the wind blow

"Hang your head over

"Hear the wind blow."

I was mesmerized. The voice was deep and gentle. At the time I had no idea what a siren's song was, but later I realized that that was exactly what I was experiencing. Had I wanted to continue on to the reservoir at that moment, I wouldn't have been able to. I was drawn to that voice every bit as powerfully as an infant is drawn to its mother's breast when hungry.

I walked up to his house and made my way to the backyard. His voice grew in volume and majesty.

"If you don't love me

"Love whom you please
"But throw your arms 'round me
"Give my heart ease
"Give my heart ease, dear
"Give my heart ease
"Throw your arms 'round me
"Give my heart ease."

I turned the corner around the side of the house and saw him hanging laundry on a line. He didn't notice me.

"Down in the valley
"Walkin' between
"Tellin' our story
"Here's what it means
"Roses love sunshine
"Violets love dew
"Angels in heaven
"Knows I love you."

I drew nearer. I sat down in the grass and crossed my legs. I stared at him as he continued to work.

"Build me a castle
"Forty feet high
"So I can see her
"As she goes by
"As she goes by, dear
"As she goes by
"So I can see her
"As she goes by
"Bird in a cage, love
"Bird in a cage
"Dyin' for freedom
"Ever a slave
"Ever a slave, dear
"Ever a slave
"Dyin' for freedom
"Ever a slave."

Benjamin hung the last piece of clothing and gathered up some stray clothes pins and his laundry basket. He noticed me for the first time, smiled, and kept singing.

"Writin' this letter

"Containin' three lines

"Answer my question

"'Will you be mine?'

"'Will you be mine, dear?'

"'Will you be mine?'

"Answer my question

"'Will you be mine?'"

He had everything gathered up by this time. "Why don't you get yourself comfortable on one of the chairs out front? I'll be right out with your lemonade."

I smiled.

He disappeared into the house with his laundry basket and clothespins. As if in a dream, I rose and walked around front. I know my feet took me around to the front of the house, but had you asked me that morning as I rocked in the chair how I ended up on his front porch, my ten-year-old mind may have answered, "I floated here."

A couple minutes later, he opened the screen door and came out with two glasses of lemonade. I was rocking slowly, peacefully.

"Ain't met a day yet I didn't like," he said.

He handed me one of the glasses and took a seat on the other rocking chair.

"You on your way to the reservoir?" asked Benjamin.

"Yeah," I answered. "I thought I'd go for a swim and do a little exploring."

"You're a regular Huck Finn, aren't you?"

I smiled and shrugged. We both took a drink of lemonade.

"Have you ever gone swimmin' down at the reservoir?" I asked him.

"No, I can't say that I have."

"You don't like swimmin'?"

"No," said Benjamin, "I like swimmin' quite a bit."

"Why don't you go?"

He thought for a moment. "The reservoir's not really a place for a man like me."

"Why not?"

"It's just not," he said softly.

"You should really go sometime – it's fun down there."

Benjamin smiled.

"I'm sure it is," he said.

"I really liked your singing," I said.

"Thank you, that's nice of you to say," replied Benjamin. "My Addie used to like to listen to me sing. It's been a while since I had an audience."

We sat silently for a while, rocking and sipping our lemonades.

"My dad doesn't like you."

"He's not the only one around here who doesn't like me," said Benjamin.

"Is it 'cause you're a nigger?" I asked.

"Yes, it's 'cause I'm a Negro."

I thought for a moment.

"That seems kinda dumb," I said. "Why would anyone care what color your skin is?"

He grinned.

"I can't say I have a good answer to that question."

"Besides, it's not your fault that Cain killed Abel," I said.

"Why do you say that?"

"Dad said you're black because Cain killed Abel and put a curse on you."

"Huh," said Benjamin, a mischievous look playing on his face. "Well, Jack, I can say with absolute certainty that you're right – I had not one thing to do with Cain killing Abel, so it's not my fault that happened."

We sat silently as I pondered my thoughts. A long moment later I said, "My dad doesn't even know you."

"Not many people around here do," said Benjamin.

I thought some more.

"I bet if my dad knew you, he'd like you." I smiled. So did Benjamin.

"Would it be okay if I used your bathroom?" I asked.

"It sure would," said Benjamin. "Just go on in the house, walk through the livin' room and back to the kitchen. The bathroom is right next to the kitchen."

"Thanks."

I got up and went into the house. I stopped just inside the door and looked around.

Benjamin's house was so different from ours. While ours was sparse – everything pretty much white-on-white, only a few pieces of furniture, a couple simple rugs – his house was lush. Not that it was extravagant, but it was inviting, as if at any point he was prepared for a whole bunch of friends and relatives to stop by, and he was going to make sure everyone felt cozy and right at home. Everything was clean and neatly organized, and it smelled of fresh-baked pie.

I turned slowly into the living room. There was a sofa, multiple rocking chairs and a comfy sitting chair, a hutch and a cabinet, and some nice things hanging on the walls. I noticed a couple hand-carved, small animals on the hutch – a fox and a frog. As I moved farther into the room I spotted two nicely-framed photos on a desk. I shifted over to take a look at them.

The first photo was of a beautiful woman. She was probably about Mom's age, maybe a little older, brown like Benjamin, in a nice dress. She had a small, playful smile on her face. This had to be Addie, Benjamin's deceased wife.

After staring at her photo for a long moment, I turned my attention to the other photo. This one was of a young man in a military uniform. He was certainly Benjamin's son. Young and strong, his smile was a mirror image of Benjamin's. I stared at the photo, captivated by it. Why would anyone hate such a happy young man? Why would anyone want him to be dead? As I stared at the photo, I had a strange sensation that I wanted to grow up to be like this man – a man I didn't even know.

I felt like I was in another world, that, like Alice, I had quickly and unexpectedly found myself somewhere strange and magical. I drifted from the living room to the dining room, but I can't recall my legs moving. It seemed I was almost outside my body, watching someone else experience the moment.

In this room were a large, formal dining table and a massive hutch. The hutch had some plates and glasses displayed on it – nothing too elaborate, yet nice. That's when I really noticed the dining room table. At one end were three place settings. I moved to the end of the table to get a better look. There, at the head of the table, was a complete place setting with plates, forks, a spoon, a knife, a cloth napkin, a glass, and a saucer with a cup. To the right and left of that setting were identical sets.

I stared at that for what seemed hours, confused at how mesmerized I was by them, at how important they seemed. Eventually I pulled myself away from the table and resumed my journey to the bathroom. As I turned to go, my eye caught something and was drawn to it. Tucked into a corner of the kitchen were an old baseball bat and glove, the glove casually hanging over the handle of the bat. I went to this coupling, drawn to it just as powerfully as Andrew Carnegie would have been drawn to a stack of hundred dollar bills.

When I neared the bat and glove, I reached my right hand out to touch them – that glove would have fit so perfectly on my left hand, that bat would have felt so majestic in my hands – but a mere inch away, my hand stopped. Slowly, I drew my hand back, aware that this wasn't just a glove and a bat, these were holy relics, sacred.

Eventually I resumed my trek to the bathroom, and a short while later I was back on the porch with Benjamin, the two of us sipping lemonade.

"You have some really nice things," I said.

"Thank you," he replied. "I appreciate you saying that."

"Are your things worth a lot?"

"More than the entire Roman empire," answered Benjamin. A dreamy look came into his eyes. "But, you know, I'd trade everything I have – every last thing – for just five more minutes with my Addie and with Jesse. To hear Addie's laugh one more time. To see the excitement on Jesse's face one more time when he's talking about the Renaissance or the Civil War. To give them both one more hug, one more kiss."

There was a smile on Benjamin's face, but I could see tears glistening in his eyes. He was quiet for nearly a minute before speaking again.

"Those things I have that are worth so much – they're only valuable because of the happiness they remind me of and the happiness they still bring me," he said.

I waited a moment.

"If I brought my baseball glove and a ball with me tomorrow, do you think we could play catch?" I asked.

His face lit up like I'd never seen before.

"I sure do," said Benjamin.

I had trouble sleeping that night. As much as I loved baseball, living out in the middle of nowhere left me few options for playing. Dad had once been an opportunity – he played catch with me a handful of times when I was five and six years old – but he was too busy now with the railroad to afford time for such luxuries. It was one of the trade-offs for making sure we had a nice place to live and food to eat. Benjamin was the only neighbor we had anywhere close to us. It wasn't as if I had a school mate close by I could play with.

Shortly after Dad left for work the next morning, I rushed down the stairs, through the living room and kitchen, hollering out, "I'm going to the reservoir!" to Mom, who was cleaning something in the dining room. I ran as fast as I could to the barn. Thirty seconds later, I had gathered up my glove and ball and hopped on my bike. I'd be at Benjamin's house in three minutes.

"Jack!" I heard Mom's voice yell out as I sped down the driveway. For a split second I kept pedaling, wondering if I could get away with pretending I hadn't heard her, but then I put the brakes on. I turned back to see her face in the kitchen window looking out at me.

"Jack, why do you have your glove with you?" she called out to me.

I didn't know what to say. Why would I have my glove with me if I was going to the reservoir? I pedaled slowly back to the window to give myself a few moments to formulate a story. I couldn't tell her the truth.

"I found this neat old brick wall down there that would be perfect for throwing the ball off so I can work on fielding grounders," I said.

"You can do that on the side of the barn," Mom said.

"Yeah, I know, but I don't want to break any boards or anything," I said. "I'd hate to make Dad have to replace a board or something or have to repaint a section of the barn because of me."

"Okay," Mom said. "I'll see you at lunch."

"All right." I turned my bike around and was back on my way to Benjamin's house.

The corn was growing quickly. Before long it would be taller than me. It went by like a blur as I barreled my way to Benjamin's.

I rode my bike up into Benjamin's yard, hopped off it, left it lying in the grass, and sprinted up to his front door. I knocked. I rocked back and forth, my weight shifting from one foot to the next, as I waited for him to answer. The door swung open moments later.

"Hi, Benjamin!" I blurted out.

His face lit up.

"How are ya, Jack?"

"I'm good." I held up my glove and ball. "You ready to play?"

"I sure am," said Benjamin. "You head on around back. I'll meet you there in just a minute or two. All right?"

I nodded my head and took off, running for the backyard.

When he emerged from the back door, he held the glove I had seen in the kitchen the day before. He slid it onto his left hand as he walked toward me. It fit his hand perfectly, naturally. Somehow, he seemed to grow twenty years younger when that glove slid onto his hand. His body moved more fluidly, wrinkles seemed to melt from his face.

"Should I go get a sponge and put it in the palm of my glove so you don't hurt my hand too badly?" Benjamin joked.

"No," I said playfully. "Where should I stand?"

"How about you stand over there in front of the barn in case I throw some wild ones." He motioned me to move maybe fifteen or twenty feet to my left. "I don't want you to have to go chasing all over the yard for any errant throws I make."

I nodded and hurried over to where he had pointed.

We began to play catch. I was nervous – so badly I wanted to make strong, accurate throws so I wouldn't embarrass myself in front of Benjamin so he'd know I was a ballplayer.

For the first couple minutes we played silently, warming our arms up slowly. He seemed to savor every catch, every throw.

"It's been a lotta years since I've done this," he eventually said.

I smiled. We continued to throw the ball back and forth. I hadn't made a bad throw yet, and I felt my nervousness dissipate. I could tell he had done this hundreds of thousands of times before. He was fluid, relaxed. Before long, it seemed as if Benjamin and I were born to play catch together. Neither of us said anything for probably close to five minutes as our arms fully loosened up, but we didn't need to say anything.

"You know, there're only three things I don't like about growin' old," he said. "Losin' my Addie, losin' my son, and not bein' able to play baseball anymore."

"Did you play in the major leagues?" I asked.

"No, but I played a lot when I was growin' up and until I was about thirty years old or so," said Benjamin. "Do you play much?"

"My friends and I would sometimes play at recess back in Churubusco."

"I bet you'll make some new friends here who'll play ball with you," Benjamin said.

"I hope so," I said.

We silently threw the ball back and forth for a while.

"What do you miss about playing baseball?" I asked. "Hitting home runs?"

"Oh, I do miss that," Benjamin said with a smile. "But back when I played, we didn't have these new balls they have today that jump off the bat like a scared rabbit, so we didn't hit too many home runs. We played what was called the inside game – lots of bunting and base stealing and hit-and-runs. No, I don't miss the home runs so much as I really miss two other things about playin' baseball."

He held the ball. A far-off look came into his eyes.

"The first one is scorin' from first base on a double. When my teammate would hit one out in the gap, and I would immediately know I had a chance to score, I'd take off runnin' as fast as I could. My hat would fly off as I rounded second, and I could feel the wind rushin' past my face as I saw the third base coach wavin' me in. I'd just keep runnin' as fast as I could, headin' for home. And as I neared the plate and I knew I was gonna score, with those last few strides I'd just glide across the plate."

He paused for a second as he closed his eyes and savored the memory.

"Mm," he finally said. "That was always somethin' special."

"What's the other thing you miss?" I asked.

"I used to play centerfield. I just loved when a batter would hit a ball way out into the alley. He'd be sure he had a double or triple. I'd take off after that ball, and I'd feel like a gazelle gallopin' across the savanna. I'd run that ball down and not just catch it, but catch it in that one perfect spot that every glove has where I wouldn't even feel the ball as it nestled in, all safe and secure, deep in my glove. Mm, that was a great feelin'."

Almost as if by magic, the years were dropping from his face. I could see the young Benjamin, as clearly as if I was watching a movie in a theater, dressed in a pinstriped uniform, speeding around the bases and flying across the outfield grass to snag a long fly ball. He was elegant, amazing.

"Can you throw me some fly balls so I can try to do that?" I asked.

"Absolutely," he said with a grin.

Benjamin threw a fly ball to me, maybe thirty feet off to my right. I ran after it with exuberance. I just missed it, but I didn't mind. I gathered up the ball and threw it back to Benjamin, ready to try again.

"You almost had it there," said Benjamin.

"Throw me another one," I said.

"You got it."

Over and over, Benjamin threw fly balls to me. I ran all over the yard trying to catch them. I missed some but caught most of them. He and I celebrated the catches and didn't worry about the misses. At first, I pretended I was Joe DiMaggio, roaming all over center field in Yankee Stadium. After a while I pretended I was Benjamin. I was running down fly balls on some long-forgotten field that had once been inhabited by the shouts and laughter and cheers of young men playing baseball for no other reason than it was the most fun they could possibly have.

This went on for at least half an hour with the two of us laughing and carrying on until he and I got tired and decided to take a break. I sat in one of the chairs under the shade tree in the backyard while he went inside to get us some refreshments. I placed the gloves and ball on the small table between the chairs and sat back, a bit of sweat perched on my forehead. The day was warm, not hot. A few clouds meandered across the sky. The tiniest of a breeze brushed my face. I didn't know if a day could be any more perfect.

Benjamin emerged from the house with a couple bottles of soda. He glided across the yard toward me. For a few seconds, I could again see the man he had been forty years earlier. When he reached me, he handed me one of the bottles.

"Here ya go," he said.

"Thanks."

He eased into the chair near me. We sat contentedly for a while.

"Did you use to play baseball with your son?"

He smiled.

"All the time," he said. "Jesse couldn't get enough of it when he was growin' up. I'd hit him grounders and fly balls and pitch batting practice to him for hours on end. For a while, he wanted to be a pitcher. I'd crouch down and catch hundreds of pitches from him. He never seemed to tire of the game."

"Was he good?" I asked.

"He sure was," said Benjamin. "He could hit and throw and run. He could do it all. But from what I saw of you today, I think you might end up bein' even better than he was."

I got a little excited.

"Really?"

"Absolutely," said Benjamin. "You have some good, soft hands, and your arm is nice and strong. Any time you want to play catch or have me throw you fly balls or ground balls, or pitch you some batting practice, you just let me know."

I smiled. He returned a playful, mischievous smile back. We both took a drink of soda.

"Have you ever seen any of the great players play, like Joe DiMaggio or Stan Musial?" I asked .

"I haven't seen those two play, but I've seen some good ones."

"Like who?"

"I lived in Chicago when I was growin' up and for a long time when I worked for the railroad," said Benjamin. "I got to see a few of the greatest players who ever played the game. You ever hear of Rube Foster?"

"No."

"Forty years ago, Rube Foster was one of the greatest pitchers in the world. He was a Negro, so he never played in the major leagues, but I saw him pitch a couple times when he was playin' with the Chicago American Giants. I can't imagine anyone ever throwin' a baseball better than he did."

"If he was so good," I asked, "why didn't he pitch in the big leagues? There are plenty of Negroes in the big leagues."

"Not back then there weren't – Negroes weren't allowed to play big league ball at that time," said Benjamin. "So the best black ballplayers back then played in the Negro Leagues and on barnstorming teams. I sure remember the first time I ever saw ol' Rube pitch. Me and two of my friends paid thirty-five cents – that was a lot of money in those days – to see Foster pitch in a game on the south side of Chicago. We got tickets for seats that were behind home plate so we could see the great Rube Foster up close and personal.

"When Rube took the mound in the top of the first inning to warm up, a huge roar went up from the crowd – there must've been five thousand people there that day. And ol' Rube started his warm ups. He threw nice and easy with a good fastball and a curve that would make any man envious. He threw a couple of his famous fadeaway pitches. So I'm there watchin' ol' Rube, and while I could see he had good stuff, it wasn't so good that I couldn't hit it, and I told my buddies that very thing. I said to them, 'If that's all Rube's got, by this time next year I'll be makin' four thousand dollars a year playin' professional Negro ball.' Now both of my friends had seen Rube pitch before, so they didn't say anything. They just looked at each other and smiled all big.

"A minute later, the game began. Two minutes after that, I knew I'd never make a penny in my life playin' professional ball. Ol' Rube would fire a fastball in there like nothin' I'd ever seen before. He'd snap off a curve that made my jaw drop. If that wasn't bad enough, he'd then turn over that fadeaway pitch of his. Boy oh boy. By the end of the first inning, I knew that if I ever played in a game against ol' Rube and batted against him four times, I'd'a struck out all four times on just twelve pitches. If I was real lucky I might work one foul tip off him. Of course, the fellas he pitched against that day didn't fare much better than I would'a – he made one batter after another look plain silly as they tried to hit him."

Benjamin was glowing with excitement at the memory. Multiple times during his tale he'd grown demonstrative, his arms moving around as if he himself was throwing a pitch or standing at the plate with a bat in his hands.

"Was he better than Lefty Grove?" I asked.

"We'll never know, but he sure was good."

"Did you ever see Babe Ruth play?"

"I sure did," answered Benjamin as a sparkle appeared in his eyes. "It was back in '21. A whole bunch of my friends and I went out to Comiskey Park one afternoon to see the great Babe Ruth play. We were sittin' way out in the upper deck of right-center field. My friends kept sayin' they hoped the Babe would hit a ball to us, and I kept tellin' 'em they were crazy. No man could possibly hit a ball far enough to reach us. If you saw where we were sittin', you'd've agreed with me. And do you know what happened?"

I excitedly shook my head.

"The Babe walloped a ball right over our heads – came down six rows *behind* us. It seemed like that ball was in the air for half an hour the way it just hung in the sky. I started thinkin' that ball might never come down. Either that or it'd end up landin' on the moon. To this day I still can't believe the Babe hit that ball that far. Boy oh boy, did my friends let me have it for sayin' Ruth couldn't hit a ball up to us, but I didn't care – I'd seen the great Babe Ruth hit one of the longest home runs in the history of the world. We talked about that home run for months."

"Wow," I said. Visions of the great Bambino walloping that home run floated through my mind as we sat silently and drank our sodas. Benjamin broke the silence.

"You know, some people said the Babe was a Negro – had to have some Negro blood in him 'cause of that nose and those lips he had. But you know what?" Benjamin locked eyes with me. "It don't matter one way or the other."

We both smiled.

"Hey," he said. "How about I get you a bat, and I'll pitch you some batting practice. Sound good?"

I felt my face light up. I nodded.

"Great," said Benjamin. "I'll be right back."

For the next hour he threw one pitch after another to me as I used the bat I had seen the day before in the kitchen. That bat sure felt good in my hands. It was a little big for me, but I choked up a bit on it so it felt just right. I'd hit the ball (I did swing and miss a few times), and one of us would go chase the ball down, then Benjamin would pitch the ball to me again. It was the best day of my life.

***

That Sunday Mom, Dad, and I went to the church in Mt. Etna. Wrapped up in a suit and tie as I sat between my parents on the seat of Dad's pickup truck, I felt as if I'd melt into a puddle of liquid flesh by the time we reached the church, what with the way the sun beat in through the windows. I contemplated asking Mom to roll down her window a little bit, but I knew she wouldn't do it because the rushing wind would mess up her hair. Dad had his window cracked open a little bit, but not so much as to ruffle her hair. The drive seemed to take forever as we wound our way through the fields and forests and over the soft hills of Huntington County. It was largely in silence, only interrupted on occasion by Mom or Dad pointing at a barn or a big house and saying, "Look at that" or "Isn't that nice," which was inevitably followed up with a "Huh" or a "Yep."

When we arrived, I could see the church was small and crowded. Men stood around and chatted outside in their shirts and ties, a few of them, like me, braving the heat with a suit coat as well. Dozens of women huddled near them, most of them wearing dress hats that I mostly found to be rather silly. Dad was in a shirt and tie, and Mom looked pretty in a floral-print dress. I was glad she wasn't wearing a hat. Staying close to her, she drifted to the gaggle of women and joined in on the conversation. Dad joined the group of men. I didn't notice him saying much.

We settled into a pew with Mom on my left and Dad on my right. The service was pretty typical – a couple hymns, announcements, a prayer, the choir belting out some song or other. Then came the sermon. Right away it became apparent that this was going to be a sermon of love and salvation. Five minutes into it, I stole a glance at my mother and could see the expected petite smile on her face. Slowly, I rotated my head to take a peek at Dad and saw exactly what I expected – a grim, dour expression on his face. Dad was a fire and brimstone, Old Testament man, and the bleeding heart sentiments of Jesus rarely resonated with him. At our old church, when Reverend Baker would sermonize on Hell and damnation, if I dared to steal a glance at my father, there would be a glint in his eyes and a tightly coiled smile on his face. On those rare occasions when Reverend Baker did speak of Jesus and love, the look on Dad's face would be one of boredom or annoyance. I knew the drive home would be contentious.

After the sermon, the offering plates were passed around. When we had gotten out of the truck after arriving, Dad had slipped a dime into my hand to put in the plate. He didn't say anything to me when he handed me the dime, but I knew what it was for. For a few seconds, I let myself fantasize about all the baseball cards that dime could buy me, but I quickly banished those thoughts as I knew if I dwelled on them too long I would become depressed. I began to wonder if that dime would go towards paying off the car the reverend drove or for helping to pay for the cost of the new roof the church would one day be putting on.

I always grew nervous as the offering plate neared me, fearing that I might drop it or that somehow the coin I had to put in it might stick to my sweaty fingers and, in my haste to get the coin in the plate before it quickly passed by, end up flicking my fingers to get the coin off them and have the coin fly off to the side, miss the plate, and clatter noisily on the tile floor. With a sigh of relief, I managed to get the dime into the plate without incident.

After the service a dozen or more people approached Mom and Dad and told them how happy they were to have met them and have them in their church. They all went out of their way to invite us back. Mom's face glowed.

On the drive home, my parents talked, their words volleyed back and forth above my head.

"So what'd you think?" Mom asked.

"I didn't care for it," answered Dad.

"Why not?"

"I didn't like the pastor. He was too timid, weak."

"I thought he was great," said Mom. "I really enjoyed his sermon. The people were so nice."

"People are nice at every church," Dad replied curtly. "We need to keep looking."

"I really liked the women there. They were very welcoming. They've already invited me to join them for the monthly bake sale."

"Every church has bake sales."

There was silence for a few seconds.

"Didn't you like the building itself, John," asked Mom. "It was pious without being pretentious."

"We need to keep looking," he said with finality, his voice a little louder, sterner.

The next ten minutes we drove in silence. I felt myself shrinking deeper and deeper into the seat, wishing I was at Benjamin's or the reservoir or anywhere else on the planet. Mom finally broke the silence, speaking with tight lips and in measured tones, staring straight forward.

"You might have the luxury of being able to take your time in finding a church because you get to interact with the men down at the rail yard five days a week. I stay at home seven days a week. I get to interact with two people – you and Jack. Every day is the same. I'm afraid that if I don't start meeting people soon I'll begin to wither."

After a brief pause Dad said, "We need to keep looking."

The rest of the drive home went by in complete silence. I felt bad for Mom. In Churubusco, she had known a lot of people since she had spent much of her life there. Even though we lived out in the country, we had neighbors who lived just a five-or ten-minute walk away. White neighbors. Here in Huntington, Benjamin was our only neighbor within close to a mile. She was marooned on an island. She needed a church to attend.

When we finally got home, I rushed up to my room, not only to shed the clothes I was trapped in, but to get away from the hostility. I stayed there for a long time, looking at the few baseball cards I had accumulated over the last handful of years, dreaming of playing in one of those distant major league cities, far from the tension-filled house where I lived. Suddenly, I couldn't wait for the beginning of the school year in another month and a half.

Chapter Two

I pedaled as fast as my legs could go, the reservoir falling farther and farther behind me. Before long, the two oaks in front of Benjamin's house began to grow bigger. Upon noticing that, I pedaled even harder.

As I neared the house I could see him on the front porch, rocking and whittling on a small piece of wood. I turned into his driveway and roared up to the porch, stopping the bike just inches short of the wooden railing. I hopped off and rushed up to Benjamin. Out of breath, I managed to get out, "The coast is clear."

His face lit up.

"Are you sure?" he asked.

I nodded excitedly, still trying to catch my breath.

Benjamin hesitated, the smile dashing from his face.

"I don't know," he said.

"Come on, it'll be fun. I promise there's no one there."

His smile returned.

"Okay. Let's go," he said.

Happily, Benjamin got up. We hurried our way around his house and to the barn. Benjamin and I swung the big doors of the barn open to reveal his 1937 Ford Woodie station wagon. Even in the shadows of the barn, I could see the car gleam.

With laughter and excitement, we hopped into the vehicle.

"You wearing your suit?" I asked.

"They're under my pants, just like you're doing," Benjamin said as he turned the ignition over and roared the car to life. "There're a couple towels in the backseat."

Benjamin threw the Woodie into gear and let out a whoop. We tore out of the barn, down the driveway, and out onto the road. Benjamin didn't even check to see if anyone was coming (no one ever was). The turn onto the dirt road sent up a hail of rocks and dust and caused me to laugh and slide across the bench seat, not stopping until my right shoulder thudded against the door.

"I can't believe I'm doing this after all these years," said Benjamin as we tore down the road.

"Do you know how to do a backstroke?" I asked.

"I sure do."

"Can you swim under water with your eyes open?"

"Yep."

"We're gonna have to have a race," I said.

"I don't know about that," replied Benjamin. "I might still know how to swim, but I don't know that I can still do it very quickly."

We exchanged a smile as the Woodie barreled along. Before we knew it, the trees surrounding the reservoir came into clear view.

"Veer to the left up there. There'll be a little opening between the trees on our right – go in through there," I said. "It's just a tiny road. You'll have to go slow on it, but after we go a little ways through the trees, we'll be there."

Benjamin followed my directions, and a moment later the water came into view. He brought the Woodie to a stop, and we looked around. We were the only people anywhere in view.

"You ready?" I asked. He nodded.

A second later we were out of the car and racing toward the water, me tearing off my shirt as I ran. Benjamin hustled along a few strides behind me.

We reached the edge of the water and stopped, ripping off our shoes and socks and pants before making our way into the welcoming water. With a shout, I began swimming, going as fast as I could. I looked back to see Benjamin make his entry into the water. His first few moments were like a sacred baptism as he almost reverently stepped into the water. He moved slowly, one foot in front of the other, until he was into the water up over his waist, the look on his face one of timidity. He stopped. After a moment's pause, a smile formed on his lips, and he dove face first into the water. When he emerged five seconds later, it was with an explosion of laughter.

"This water feels so good," he said after he caught his breath. "For so many reasons."

For the next twenty minutes we laughed and swam and frolicked like a couple ten year olds. Benjamin accepted my challenge to a race. I won easily and laughed and laughed when he showed me how he could do a handstand in the water, his legs wiggling frantically about as he tried to maintain his balance for an extra couple seconds.

Soon we found ourselves lazing about in the shallow water so he could relax a little and catch his breath. He was a little tired but a lot happy.

"Tell me a story about Addie," I said. His face lit up.

"I'd be happy to," said Benjamin. He thought, a studious look momentarily on his face, but the big smile soon returned.

"Here's one for ya. You know, back when the Great Depression hit, my Addie and Jesse and I had a little house in Chicago not far from the rail yard. Times sure were tough, but we managed to survive it okay, much better than a lot of people. My Addie, any time we had an extra dollar or two, why, she'd go to the store and get all the fixin's to make a couple loaves of bread and a pie or two, and she'd bake up some fresh bread. She'd make a whole mess of peanut butter and honey sandwiches and cheese sandwiches, and she'd bake up a couple pies. She'd wrap those sandwiches and slices of pie up in paper, put 'em in a picnic basket, and send Jesse down to the tracks to hand out the food to the men who were tramping about the country, just tryin' to survive.

"Before long, word got out where we lived. These men would sometimes come to our house and knock on the door and ask if we could spare them a little food. My Addie never once turned one of these men away. Why, sometimes she gave away just about every bit of food we had in the house. There were plenty of times I walked into the kitchen to see her sittin' at the table and talkin' with a strange man who was eatin' a big bowl of her vegetable soup and drinkin' a glass of lemonade or enjoyin' a nice slice of pie and a warm cup of coffee. If it was breakfast time, she'd fry 'em up some eggs and make 'em a couple slices of toast loaded with butter and sugar and cinnamon on it. Sometimes it was a white man, and sometimes it was a black man sittin' there. Hunger sure does go a long way toward folks not worryin' one way or the other what color someone's skin is.

"One time Jesse, who was just a boy at the time, asked my Addie, 'Momma, why do you give all our food away all the time?' She said to him, 'Times are tough, Jesse. We got it better than most. It's our duty to help out those who ain't got it so good. Those are good people who are just down on their luck right now. If you were in their position, wouldn't you hope that others would share their food with you?' Jesse smiled and nodded and never said another word about it. There were times when she'd given away all the food we had in the house but a little bread and butter, and we'd sit around the table at night, eatin' our dinner of tea and toast. I'd look across the table at my Addie, and I couldn't help but smile to know that such a wonderful woman had chosen to cast her lot with me. I sure was a lucky man, Jack."

I could tell by the look on his face he really meant this. I was happy for him.

"Maybe we should get goin' – we don't wanna push our luck," Benjamin said a moment later.

We finished up long before we wanted to, gathered together our shirts and shoes and pants, and went back to the Woodie. We dried ourselves quickly before getting in the car and said little on the drive home as we simply reveled in the enjoyment we'd just had. At one point, I looked over at Benjamin to see his face beaming with happiness.

Later that day, we found ourselves rocking contentedly on his front porch. Two plates, both empty except for some crumbs, sat on the little table between us, forks resting listlessly on their edges. Two swimsuits and two towels, draped over the porch railing, were nearly dry. We sipped some lemonade as twilight eased its way in.

"Can I get you another slice of pie?" Benjamin asked me.

"No, thanks. I'm stuffed."

"You sure your parents aren't worried about you?"

"Nah. I told 'em I wanted to get a good look at the stars tonight and would be back a little after dark."

Benjamin nodded.

"I had a really fun day today," he said.

"Me, too."

"Thanks, Jack."

"You're welcome," I said with a smile. We rocked in silence, looking out over the corn fields as the sky turned various shades of red.

"One of life's sweetest pleasures is comin' our way," Benjamin said.

I looked up and down the road.

"Where?" I asked.

"Everywhere you look."

I was confused.

"I don't see anything," I said. Benjamin grinned.

"Your mother ever tuck you in bed at night?" he asked.

"Sometimes."

"Doesn't that give you a nice, warm feelin' all inside?"

"Yeah," I said.

"Nightfall is my mother. Every day she comes along and gradually dims the light. She pulls that big dark blanket up to my neck and turns on those millions of tiny lights that make the whole world beautiful and pure. Why, after bein' tucked in like that, it's impossible not to have a wonderful night's sleep."

I smiled as he and I looked out on the darkening fields and quietly rocked.

"Yep," said Benjamin. "There's nothin' quite like sittin' with your best friend late on a quiet afternoon and waiting for evening to come."

He looked contentedly out over the fields. I glanced at him and smiled even more. After a few moments, I returned my attention to the fields. We rocked in blissful silence, the only sounds the gentle, rhythmic creakings of the chairs moving forward and back and the happy crickets chirping away.

Having been up so late that night, the next morning I slept in a little later than normal. When I finally awoke I saw it was already nearly 6:30. I could hear Dad moving around the house, getting ready for work. I laid in bed, not moving, staring out the window at the bright sunlight. Ten minutes later, I heard the screen door of the kitchen slam closed, and just after that I heard his truck start up. It rumbled by below my window a few seconds later. I got out of bed.

After washing up, I went to the kitchen. Mom was waiting for me.

"Good morning, sleepyhead," she said.

"Hi, Mom."

"Go ahead and sit down there. I'll have your breakfast ready in a moment."

I sat down.

"Did you see lots of stars last night?" she asked.

"Yes, ma'am. I couldn't believe how many there were. I even picked out the Big Dipper."

"Good for you."

She shoveled some potatoes and eggs out of the frying pan and onto a couple plates. She came over to the table with them. She placed one in front of me and sat down across the table from me with her plate.

"I mailed off a letter yesterday to your Uncle Bob and Aunt Sadie to see if they might come for a visit," Mom said.

My face brightened.

"Really? Do you think they'll come?"

"We'll see."

I hoped they'd come see us. Aunt Sadie made the best mashed potatoes I'd ever had. Uncle Bob had once lived in New York City for a little while. I loved hearing him tell stories of New York, which seemed as if it was a million miles away from Indiana. I couldn't believe so many people lived in one place. Uncle Bob also knew how to play card games like 1-2-3, Casino, and I Win – You Lose. We'd play each other for hours, betting a penny a hand. Mom didn't like that I was betting. Even though he always took every penny I had, after he and Aunt Sadie would leave, I'd find not only all my pennies left behind in a bowl for me but all of his pennies as well, plus a few nickels and dimes. There were many times I found myself wishing he was my father.

Mom and I ate in silence for a little bit before I spoke again. I picked my words carefully.

"What makes Negroes so different from us?"

Her face quickly snapped up from staring down at her food, and her eyes locked on mine. I immediately caught my mistake in word choices – the only word we'd ever used in our house to refer to black people was a different N word.

"Why do you ask?" Her eyes stayed locked on mine. Her lips seemed to barely move.

"I'm just wondering because I see that guy down the road all the time when I'm going to the reservoir. He always waves to me, like a nice person would do."

"There are some people you just can't trust, Jack. People like him, they do some rude, disrespectful things that we want no part of."

"Like what?" I asked, making sure my voice didn't take on an accusatory or confrontational tone.

"The men of those people are always trying to do… inappropriate things with women like me. Things that are wrong and disgusting. The way they worship our Lord is blasphemous. Worshiping is a solemn, sacred event, but those people shout and yell and dance when they're in church. It's an abomination how they act. You can't trust those kind of people."

I nodded and went back to my food. Mom could tell I wasn't completely sold on her explanation. She tried another approach.

"Do you remember earlier this summer when we drove into Fort Wayne to attend the picnic the railroad threw for its employees?"

"Yeah," I answered.

"Do you remember how that one awful man there kept talking about the war on poverty and the socialist revolution?" she asked.

I did remember, not because I knew what either of those things were, but because the phrases involved the words "war" and "revolution." I was confused by how they tied in with "poverty" and "socialist," those words completely foreign to me.

"Yes."

"Someone like that," Mom said, "even though they're white, is not to be trusted either. Some people are to be avoided and disliked because of how they act and what they believe. Now finish your breakfast."

I did as told.

A couple days later, Benjamin and I found ourselves in his garden. We weren't working very hard as we pulled an occasional weed and generally just fussed about.

"Everything looks like it's coming in real nice," I said.

"Yeah, we've sure been fortunate this summer," replied Benjamin.

Some cherry tomatoes suddenly caught my eye. I moved to them.

"These look awfully good," I said.

"Have yourself some."

I turned and looked at him.

"Really? I can?"

"Sure, that's what they're there for," said Benjamin. "To be eaten. A vegetable or a piece of fruit never tastes better than in that moment right after it's been picked."

I plucked a cherry tomato off the vine and popped it into my mouth.

"That is so good," I said.

"Isn't it, though? Have some more."

I threw a few more cherry tomatoes into my mouth. Benjamin smiled as he watched me before returning to tending the garden. As I ate a fifth and a sixth tomato, he made his way to some okra.

"This okra sure is lookin' good," he said. "Jack, come on over here and try some of this."

As I moved over toward Benjamin, he picked a couple okras off the plant and handed one of them to me. We both bit into the okra.

"Oh, isn't that good?" said Benjamin.

"It's so sweet."

"No cooking needed. Have all you want," said Benjamin.

As I continued to eat, Benjamin went back to tending some of the plants. He talked as he worked.

"When Jesse was a boy and we still lived in Chicago, my Addie always kept a beautiful little vegetable garden out back. Any time during the summer that I lost track of Jesse, all I had to do was go on out there to the garden, and there I'd find him, eatin' okra and snap peas and cherry tomatoes and anything he could get his hands on." There was a look of joy on Benjamin's face.

As I kept eating the okra, shocked at how good it tasted, I could understand why Jesse would lose himself in the garden.

Benjamin continued to work in the garden as I kept on eating. Before long, I found myself filling up a bit, and I took a break.

"Hey, Benjamin," I said. "You wanna play some baseball?"

A big smile appeared on his face.

"You don't have to ask me twice."

We started walking up to the house to get the bat and ball and gloves.

"Do you wanna hit first?" I asked.

"Okay," Benjamin answered with a gleam in his eyes.

We had begun playing each other in one-on-one games. I always won. While I knew it was because I was younger and could run faster than Benjamin, I also knew it was partly because he would make sure I won by occasionally trying to take an extra base when he knew I'd be able to run him down and tag him out. Sometimes, he would take a little longer to run down a ball I'd hit than it should have, giving me time to round the bases for a home run. I loved Benjamin for this.

When we'd gotten the equipment, we took our places on our field behind his house. Whoever was batting laid their glove down for home plate, a well-coiffed bush served as first base, one of the yard chairs or a section of newspaper with a rock on it would serve as second base, and the trunk of a small tree served as third.

Benjamin readied himself to hit. He tapped the bat on the plate.

"Fire one in here, Jackie," he said. "Let me see that fastball of yours."

I stared in at an invisible catcher, gritted my teeth, went into my windup, and fired in a pitch that was a good two feet outside.

"Sorry," I called out as Benjamin chased the ball down.

"Don't you worry about it," he called over a shoulder. "Pitches get away from all of us sometimes."

He threw the ball back to me. I readied for the next pitch. I took a little off that one to increase its chances of going over the plate, which it did. While his movement wasn't as quick and explosive as it surely once had been, Benjamin put a beautiful swing on the ball and hit it out into left-center field. I took off after it.

"I got all of that one!" Benjamin took off for first base.

The ball rolled all the way out to the barn, coming to rest near the big doors at the front. I sprinted as fast as I could, glancing back over my shoulder to see him ambling around the bases.

I reached the ball and looked up to see Benjamin heading for second base. I took off running after him. Had we been playing a more competitive game, he would have stopped at second and announced that there was now a ghost runner on second base as he went up to take his next at bat, but he kept running, rounding second and heading for third. I had little trouble catching him before he reached third. I ran past him and lightly tagged him out. We both laughed with joy.

"You're a regular Cool Papa Bell," Benjamin said. "The way you can run all over the field."

"Who's that?"

Benjamin took a moment to catch his breath.

"Cool Papa was one of the all-time greats in the Negro Leagues. He could really hit and field, but he was mainly known for his speed. Boy, was he fast. The guys who played with Cool Papa said he was so fast that when they were on the road and staying in a hotel room, Cool Papa could flip off the light switch by the door of the room and be all tucked into bed before the room went dark."

"No way!" I exclaimed.

"That's what they said," said Benjamin.

"Wow," I said. "And I'm as fast as he is?"

"Not yet – ol' Cool Papa was a grown man when he was at his fastest. Maybe one day you'll be as fast as he was."

I couldn't help but smile. Recently I had noticed that I typically smiled more in two hours with Benjamin than I did in an entire month with my parents.

"Gimme your glove," he said. "You go on up and take a few swings."

"Okay," I said with excitement.

I handed Benjamin my glove and the ball and raced up to the plate to bat. He took his place in the middle of the diamond and prepared to pitch.

"You ready, Jack?"

"Can you call me 'Cool Papa'?"

A huge smile flooded over his face.

"You got it, Cool Papa."

I tapped the bat on the plate and took my stance, my face beaming.

"Fire one in here!" I called out.

Benjamin went into his windup and threw a perfect pitch right down the middle. I swung as hard as I could and hit a long fly ball to center field.

"Great swing, Cool Papa!" Benjamin yelled out as I took off running. He scampered off after the ball as I tore around the bases. I ran as fast as I could, pretending I was the great Cool Papa Bell.

As I rounded second base, Benjamin was just getting to the ball. I knew he would never be able to catch me and that I had an easy home run, but I didn't slow down, trying my hardest to run as fast as Cool Papa.

Benjamin was just getting back into the infield as I crossed home plate. As I slowed down, he let out a cheer and raised his hands in celebration. He was even happier than I was.

That night it took me a long time to fall asleep. It was my own fault. I had brushed my teeth and changed into my pajamas and should have been able to just hop in bed and go to sleep. As I stood by the door and prepared to flip off the light switch, thoughts of Cool Papa Bell floated through my head. My hand rested on the switch, my bed just eight feet away. I took a deep breath, then flipped the switch – before I'd even moved, the room was dark. I turned the light back on. I took another breath, flipped the switch, and bolted for my bed. The room was long dark as I leapt onto the bed. I scrambled back to the light switch.

This process repeated itself a dozen times or more before Mom appeared at the top of the stairs. She stared at me with a confused look on her face.

"Jack, what're you doing?"

"I'm trying to tuck myself into bed before the room goes dark," I answered.

"Why would you be trying to do that?"

I froze. I couldn't tell Mom about Cool Papa because she'd know where I'd heard about him. I didn't know what to say. Then something sprang to mind.

"To see if I can be like Superman," I quickly said. "I figure if I can be faster than light, I'll be at least as fast as a speeding bullet."

Mom was bemused.

"That's enough of trying to be like Superman tonight. Get into bed."

"Yes, ma'am."

I turned off the light, walked to my bed, and got under the covers. She watched as I snuggled myself under the blanket.

"Good night, Jack."

"Good night, Mom."

She walked off. I laid there for over an hour and visualized Cool Papa zipping his way around the bases, causing havoc on the field, disrupting his opponents. I pictured myself doing the same thing in a few years at Wrigley Field, leading the Cubs to their first World Series title in fifty years. I'd be a hero in Chicago. Kids all over the country would love me. By the time I drifted off to sleep, I was deliriously happy.

The next night, I couldn't fall asleep for a long time either, but it was for a very different reason.

Mom, Dad, and I were gathered in the living room after supper. Dad was listening to the radio as Mom read a book. I was on the floor reading the comics and the sports page. Dad looked up at the clock on the wall.

"It's gettin' late, Jack," said Dad. "You better head on up to bed."

"Yes, sir."

I quickly and neatly folded up the paper, got up, placed it in the magazine rack, and started to leave the room.

"Come give me a kiss," Mom said.

I changed course and went over to her, giving her a quick kiss on the cheek.

"Sleep well," she said.

"Okay," I replied.

I headed off, turning the corner to make my way to the stairs. Just before I reached the stairs I noticed my socks were falling down. I pulled them up, wanting to make sure I didn't slip because of them. As I fiddled with my socks, I heard Dad speak.

"You think he's been spendin' time over at that nigger's house?" he asked Mom.

There was a pause as I heard her place her book down on the little stand by her chair. I silently slipped back toward the living room.

"I don't think so," she said.

"He goes right past that house every day when he goes to the reservoir," Dad said. "Why would that old nigger have bought a house around here anyway? It's gettin' so those people are everywhere. Doesn't he know his place?"

"Jack's a good boy," Mom said. "I'm sure he's paying heed to what you told 'im."

"He better be, but I have my doubts."

She stayed quiet. After a moment I made a move to start back toward the stairs when I heard Dad speak again.

"I can't believe the things that're goin' on in this world anymore."

"Like what?"

"We had a train from Cleveland stop in the rail yard today," said Dad. "One of the guys on it said niggers are marryin' white women all over Cleveland."

"They are?"

"Can you imagine?" he asked.

"It's sad," she said. "The world sure is changing."

"Not for the better," replied Dad. "This entire country is goin' to Hell because of the niggers. There's little we can do about it." He paused for a moment. "I'm gettin' really tired of niggers gettin' all the breaks and all kinds of handouts and ruinin' this country for good, hard-workin' people like us."

I stood silently, afraid to move. My parents were both quiet for a few long moments. I had just begun to force myself to step softly back to the stairs when my father spoke again.

"You know, I'm not gonna say we didn't need to stop Hitler, but I'm also not gonna say he was completely wrong in everything he believed."

My father went silent. Mom was quiet.

"There's something to be said for racial purity," my father eventually added.

Mom said nothing.

As quietly as I could, I snuck to the stairs and climbed them carefully to make sure none of the stairs squeaked. I made it to my room and climbed softly into bed. There would be no Cool Papa antics that night.

The next morning I left the house and went to Benjamin's. As I approached his place I turned my head around to make sure no one was on the road behind me – it was clear, no traffic at all. I turned into his driveway and made sure I went all the way behind his house before getting off my bike and parking it. A wave of joy flooded over me when I spotted him sitting under the shade tree as he whittled. I walked quickly toward him.

"Hiya, Jack," Benjamin called out to me.

"Hey, Benjamin." I immediately felt better, the awful words of the night before drifting away. "Whatcha makin' this time?"

"A dog."

"What kind?"

"I haven't decided yet," Benjamin answered. "Maybe a Jack Russell."

I sat down in the chair next to him and watched him work.

"Can I get you anything?" Benjamin asked as he looked up at me.

"No," I said, "I'm good."

I watched him carve for a minute. His hands worked so smoothly, so deftly on the wood, the small pocketknife seeming like just another finger on his hand. I had never seen anyone whittle besides him, but I knew he had to be a master at what he was doing.

"That's amazing," I suddenly heard myself say.

"Thank you, Jack." Benjamin whittled for another moment before glancing at me. "You wanna give it a try?" He held the wood and the pocketknife toward me.

"I'd like to try, but I don't wanna ruin your dog," I said.

"Don't you worry about that," said Benjamin. "For all we know, you'll make it an even better dog."

He put the wood and the pocketknife into my hands and scooted his chair closer to me.

"You've been watchin' me, so you have an idea what to do," said Benjamin. "Simply try to see the dog in the wood. After that, all you have to do is remove all the wood that's gettin' in the way of us seein' that dog."

I stared at the wood, but I couldn't see much of a dog in it. I made a few tentative cuts, trying to move smoothly as Benjamin did.

"That's right," said Benjamin. "Always move the blade away from ya as you're learnin'."

I made a couple more tentative cuts.

"There ya go, that's better," said Benjamin.

"But I'm so slow."

"That's okay. It's not a race to get finished. Enjoy every step of the journey."

Meticulously, I continued to carve on the wood for a short while before stopping.

"Did Jesse know how to carve?" I asked.

"Yep. He was pretty good at it, too."

I worked a little more on the wood, focusing even harder on what I was doing.

"Do you think he and I would be friends if he was still alive?" I asked.

"I'm sure you two would be the best of friends."

Benjamin smiled. I did the same.

"I think we would be, too," I said.

I went back to carving the wood. I began to feel slightly more comfortable with the wood and knife in my hands as Benjamin kept a close watch over me.

"Tell me more about Addie," I found myself saying.

I looked up from the wood to see his face light up.

"Oh, my Addie. She was somethin' special. How she could make me laugh. She may have been the funniest person I ever met. She was always so happy and positive. She always said that no matter how bad a person someone might seem to be, if you looked hard enough, you'd find something beautiful and wonderful about them. She was convinced that even with the most hardened murderer who's going to spend the rest of their life in prison, if you spoke with them long enough and really got to know them, you'd be able to find at least one thing to love about 'em. And, you know, after hearing my Addie explain her thoughts on this so passionately and with so much compassion, I couldn't help but agree with her." Benjamin paused, his face still ebullient. "Everyone loved bein' around her. Boy, could she cook. Everything I liked, she could make, and she always made it better than anyone else did. You haven't lived until you've had my Addie's peach pie. Mm mm. And she was so pretty – to this day she's the prettiest woman I ever met. Every day with her was like Christmas Day – a treasure, a gift." A bit of the luster left his face. "But when we got the word that Jesse had been killed, well… she was never the same afterwards. She was so sad. Her heart was broken beyond repair. She tried to hang in there. I did everything I could think of to cheer her up, to bring her back to me, but I never did find that thing that worked. My Addie tried to laugh, she tried to carry on, but the hurt was just too much for her gentle soul. She died barely a year after Jesse did."

"I'm sorry."

"Don't be." The smile returned to Benjamin's face. "Few people have ever gotten to experience the happiness my Addie and I shared. I got to experience thirty-five years of heaven bein' with her. I like to think she had a pretty good time as well."

"I wish I'd had the chance to know her," I said.

"You'd've liked her. I'm sure she would've liked you, too. I'm just thankful I had the time with her that I did, just like I'm thankful for the time I have with you."

I blushed. He smiled.

"I know," Benjamin said.

That Saturday morning I was rushing about to get ready to go to Benjamin's house. We'd made plans to play a full nine-inning baseball game against each other. I couldn't wait to get started. He always had something delicious waiting for me when I arrived. Saturdays were often oatmeal raisin cookie day, and his were better than anything else I'd ever eaten. Of course, with our baseball game each half inning would consist of just one out instead of three so he didn't get too tired. That was okay with me – I'd be doing my favorite thing with my favorite person. But my joy and excitement came to an abrupt end.

"Get yourself out to the truck, Jack," Dad called out from downstairs as I sat on the edge of my bed and tied my sneakers. "We're goin' into town to pick up some things."

My heart dropped. My feet filled with lead.

I sat on the bed's edge, paralyzed. My mind started scrambling, trying to think of some way to get out of the trip into town, but no reasonable excuse came to mind. I was trapped.

A minute later I shuffled into the kitchen to find Mom tidying things up. She spoke without looking at me.

"You ready to go?" Mom asked.

"Yes, ma'am," I said. "What are we goin' into town to get?"

"We need to get you some clothes for school, and your dad needs to get some things at the hardware store."

"So we won't be gone too long then?"

"Probably an hour or so," Mom answered.

My baseball game with Benjamin would be delayed, but not cancelled. My heart lightened a tiny bit.

We sat three abreast in the cab of Dad's pickup truck. The drive into town was quiet for the first few minutes until he spoke.

"Are you lookin' forward to school startin'?" he asked me.

"Yes, sir."

"Maybe you'll be able to make some friends who don't live too far away who you can play with," Mom said.

"Maybe," I replied.

A short while later we pulled up in front of Woolworth's. Dad handed some money to Mom.

"I'll meet you both back here in half an hour," he said.

Mom and I got out of the truck and went into the store. We found some clothes that I needed – some underwear and socks, a couple shirts (which Mom held up against my back to see if they'd fit), and a pair of pants – and made our way to the register. As we waited in line I scanned the candy display. There were dozens of different kinds of candy bars and gum and other candy. Tucked in alongside the candy were some packs of baseball cards. I looked at the baseball cards with longing, wondering whose cards might be hidden within the packs. Maybe there was a

Hank Sauer card or maybe a Yogi Berra, who I liked even though he played for the Yankees and not the Cubs. I caught myself dreaming of what it would be like to play a game in Yankee Stadium, running down a deep fly ball way out in Death Valley in left-centerfield, robbing an unsuspecting batter of what he was sure was going to be a triple as fifty thousand fans cheered for me. I'd make the long jog to the dugout, the cheers ringing in my ears, my teammates slapping me on the back for the great play I'd just made.

"Would you like a pack?" Mom said, jolting me out of my reverie.

"Yes, ma'am," I said excitedly as I felt a large smile flood over my face.

Mom reached down and grabbed one of the packs.

"Is this one okay?" she asked.

I nodded my head. I was still smiling. She smiled back at me.

We stood outside Woolworth's and waited for my father. Mom handed me the pack of cards out of the shopping bag. I opened it. There wasn't a Hank Sauer or a Yogi Berra card in the pack, but I was excited to find a card of Bob Rush, the Cubs' best pitcher. Dad pulled up a moment later as I scoured the cards. Mom and I got into the truck.

"Did you find everything you needed?" Dad asked.

"We did," Mom answered.

Dad turned his attention to me.

"I picked up something from the hardware store for you," he said.

"You did?" I grew excited. For the life of me I couldn't figure out what I could use from the hardware store. "What is it?"

"It's back there," Dad said with a jerk of his thumb to the bed of the truck. I turned, raised myself up against the back of the seat, and looked into the bed of the truck. All I saw were a whole bunch of cans of paint.

"Paint?" I asked.

"Yeah," Dad said. "You're gonna paint the shed."

I sat back down.

"But I don't know how to paint," I said.

"You'll figure it out," Dad said.

I looked at Mom – she was gazing out the window, and she kept her scrutiny in that direction.

How was I going to paint the shed? The shed was nearly the size of a small house. I'd never painted anything before other than occasionally doing some painting on paper during our art lessons at school.

"When should I start?" I asked.

"You'll start when we get home," said Dad.

I was devastated. My heart sank again.

As we drove home my mind raced. Would it take me all day to paint the shed? Two days? A month? I had no idea. Was I supposed to paint for a couple hours a day or all day long? What if I did a lousy job or messed up and got paint on things I wasn't supposed to get paint on? Would Dad give me a whipping?

When we got home Dad unloaded one can of paint after another out of the back of the truck as Mom hurried inside with my clothes and baseball cards.

"I want it painted red with white trim," Dad said. He handed me a single paintbrush, which was only about an inch and a half wide. "Here's your brush. Get to work."

He walked into the house. I stared down at all the paint. I not only didn't know how to paint, I didn't even know how to get the lids off the cans.

Two hours later I had barely gotten going on the shed, and I was very confused. I was spreading the red paint with my small brush on the east side of the shed, but the paint sure wasn't making the shed look very red. The paint was very pale, almost pink, and it seemed really oily.

After a while, I convinced myself that the paint simply went on looking pink, and that when it dried it would turn red, but as the day wore on and I kept smearing paint on the shed, I'd look back at the parts I'd painted hours earlier to see that it was dry, but it looked every bit as pale as when I had first put it on. That's when I noticed, as my gaze followed the trail of where I had started painting to where I stood, that the paint was slowly getting slightly darker. I looked down into the can of paint – the paint was starting to look red. When I picked up the can to get a closer look the paint sloshed around just a tiny bit, and I noticed the paint that was down a little lower in the can was even redder. My confusion grew.

I put the can down and went to the barn to find something I could use to check deeper down into the can. I went to Dad's work bench and found a metal rod that was maybe a foot and a half long. I took the rod to the can of paint and plunged it in. I noticed the paint was really thick down at the bottom of the can – I had to strain a little to force the rod to the very bottom of the can. When I pulled the rod back out of the paint, the color of the paint that was stuck on the bottom of the rod was of blood. It suddenly struck me – I should have stirred the paint first, and I had just wasted the last three hours.

As I put the lid back on that can of paint, got the next can, took the lid off it, and began to stir it, I realized just how miserable I was. I was thirsty, hungry, tired, and hot. Mostly I was lonely as I wondered what Benjamin was doing. I longed for the baseball game that he and I were supposed to play and the joy and laughter we were supposed to share.

It wasn't until midafternoon that Mom emerged from the house with a sandwich and a glass of milk.

"Why didn't you come in for lunch?" she asked as she handed the plate with the sandwich on it to me.

"I didn't know I was allowed to come in," I answered as I grabbed the plate and took a greedy bite of the sandwich, peanut butter and jelly never tasting so good.

"Of course you can come in. It's not like you're being punished."

It sure felt as if I was.

A couple hours later I went inside to eat supper. Mom, Dad, and I sat around the kitchen table.

"How's it coming?" Dad asked.

"Okay," I answered. I had no idea if things were going well or not.

"You makin' good progress?"

I'd gotten a few feet of the east side of the shed painted, and that didn't include the higher reaches of the side which I couldn't reach – tomorrow I'd get the ladder out so I could reach those spots.

"Some," I answered.

"Huh," Dad replied.

When supper was over I went back out and resumed my work. I painted in silence, the only sounds the whisper of the paint brush as it glided along the shed's wall and the gradually encroaching chirping of that evening's crickets. The shadows had grown long when Dad appeared at the back door.

"Get your things put away and get yourself ready for bed," he called out.

"Yes, sir," I answered. I didn't know if I said it loud enough for him to hear or not.

The next day was more of the same. I began painting early in the morning, even before Mom and Dad had gotten up and about. The amount of progress I made was minimal. The brush was so small that I'd work for an hour, step back, and hardly be able to tell that I'd accomplished anything, typically having managed to get only a couple slats painted. Every couple hours Mom would come out with a glass of water or milk or maybe a sandwich and ask how I was doing. I'd mumble "Fine" or "Okay" and continue working.

I realized on that Sunday that I better keep myself in the shade as much as possible or I'd bake like a potato in the sun. I began to paint only areas that were in the shade. That meant leaving off on one side to move to a different side when the sun started beating down on me. At one point, I took a minute to survey my work, walking a slow lap around the shed. I almost laughed out loud when I saw the haphazard work I had done. I knew at that point that the job would take me even longer than I had imagined to complete. I got the sinking feeling that I'd still be painting the shed even after school started in September.

While Mom came out every now and then to bring me something to eat or drink, Dad never said a thing to me the entire day. A couple times he went to the barn, but he didn't acknowledge me.

Mom called me in for dinner. She told me to wash up first. When I saw myself in the mirror, I could see red paint all over me. I contemplated making Indian noises by tapping on my open mouth while I hummed, but I was afraid Dad might hear me, think I was having fun, and get mad.

After a largely silent dinner where the only talking consisted of Dad telling a story that proved what an idiot he thought his boss was, I asked if I could be excused from the table. When Mom said I was, I headed for the back door.

"I think you've painted enough for today, Jack," she said.

"That's okay," I replied. "I can still work a little longer."

I went out the door, making sure the screen didn't slam behind me. The sooner I finished painting the shed, the quicker Benjamin and I would be able to play our baseball game.

The next morning I had already been painting for half an hour when Dad came out of the house. My back stiffened as I continued to work. He fiddled around in the barn for a couple minutes, then finally got in the pickup truck and headed off for the rail yard. I exhaled.

The red parts on the shed grew slightly larger as the morning wore on. At one point Mom came out of the house with some wet clothes to hang up to dry. She called out to me. I gave her a small wave.

She hung the clothes in silence. A short while later I heard her footsteps moving across the gravel of the driveway, the screen door banged shut, and I was again left alone to do my work

I worked mindlessly, my right hand moving up and down in front of me, the only slightly-faded shed becoming a little bit redder. I had worked for a while without a single thought seemingly flitting through my mind when I suddenly heard a far-off cough. I snapped out of my trance and looked down the driveway toward the road – my heart soared. There was Benjamin, framed between the tall stalks of corn on one side and the edge of the house on the other, sauntering slowly by as casually as someone out on a Sunday stroll. He didn't look at me, but he gave me the tiniest of nods. I had a new hero.

A moment later, he was out of view, but the image of him walking by, and the knowledge that he cared about me as much as I cared about him, filled me with joy. I worked with new vigor.

A little while later, I heard a loud, fake sneeze and looked down the driveway to see Benjamin strolling along on the other side of the road, his head facing straight ahead as it had to. I was not alone.

Around noon, Mom called me in for lunch. When I entered the kitchen, with plenty of paint on my arms and face, she already had a sandwich and a glass of milk on the table for me. She had half a sandwich on a plate for herself.

"Go wash up, okay?" she said when I tromped in through the screen door.

"Yes, ma'am."

A minute later we were both sitting at the table and eating.

"You should come down to the reservoir with me some time," I said between bites. "It's a lot of fun there. Maybe we could go swimming or hiking or something."

"I wish I could," Mom replied. "But there's always so much work to do around here between washing the clothes and cleaning the dishes and sweeping the floors and dusting and all."

"Maybe some morning I could help you get all your work done. We could go in the afternoon after lunch."

"Maybe," Mom said. "We'll see."

We both took a bite of food. I chewed and swallowed a mouthful.

"Why does Dad hate black people so much?"

"It's not that he hates 'em," Mom said, her voice soft. "It's that he realizes... that we have to be careful around 'em. You just never know what a black person might do. They're not like us."

This sounded like it was going to be the same explanation I heard a couple weeks earlier, but I pressed on to see if something new might come out.

"They're not?"

"No," Mom said. "They're lazy and dirty and not very smart. They don't have the morals that we have. I'm not saying every one of 'em is like that. For example, some black people are Negroes. They keep to themselves, they behave well, and they know their place in society. But most black people are niggers, the ones who are loud and belligerent and don't know how to behave themselves in public and who use drugs and don't know their proper place in society. Those are the ones you really have to be careful around." She went quiet for a moment as she collected her thoughts. "Niggers are at the bottom of the barrel. All they want to do is drag everyone else down with them to the very bottom. Even if you try to help them up, more than likely they'll drag you down to their level. Let's talk about something else. Are you excited for school to be starting in a few weeks?"

"No."

"Why not? The other day you were excited for it to start."

"I've been having fun this summer," I said. "When school starts, I won't have time to do all the fun things I've been doing."

"You'll still have weekends for going down to the reservoir. Think of all the new friends you'll soon be making."

I finished chewing the bite of sandwich in my mouth and swallowed it. "I guess."

I took another bite. After I swallowed I asked, "Any word yet on if Uncle Bob and Aunt Sadie can come for a visit?"

Mom shook her head.

"They're busy right now. They won't be able to come see us."

I was starting to figure out that life didn't always go as we hoped it would.

I painted the rest of that day in silence. The next morning was more of the same – until I heard a familiar cough. Only this time the cough occurred while Benjamin was still obscured by the corn stalks. He never looked my way, but at the very edge of the corn field, at the base of the driveway, I saw him drop something. I couldn't tell what it was. When it hit the ground, it disappeared in the tufts of wild grass growing there. He walked on without so much as a nod.

My mind raced. What had Benjamin dropped for me? Should I run and get it now? What if Mom saw me down at the end of the driveway? She would surely ask what I was up to – if not immediately, then at least when we sat down for lunch.

I had to find out what Benjamin left for me. I kept painting as I weighed the odds. Mom wasn't always at the kitchen window doing dishes or rinsing something off or preparing a meal, but she sure was there a lot. I had noticed her looking out the screen door to check on me a few times since I'd started on the shed. But she also spent time cleaning in other parts of the house, or sometimes sat for a while and drank some sun tea and listened to the radio as she took a break.

I decided to feign thirst and go into the kitchen to scout things out. I entered the deserted kitchen and walked quietly to the sink, listening for her movements around the house. All was quiet. I reached the sink, grabbed my glass, and filled it with water. I began to drink, and that's when I finally heard something – Mom was upstairs, and she was pulling the vacuum cleaner out of the closet.

I dallied by the sink, sipping on the water, waiting for the whir of the vacuum to commence. I put my glass back on the counter by the sink and waited. Finally, the vacuum roared to life. With that, I bolted for the back door, closed it softly behind me to be safe, and sprinted around the house and down the driveway to find the treasure that awaited me.

When I reached the end of the driveway I quickly scoured the grass. It didn't take long to find my reward – a small, brown paper bag with four of Benjamin's thick, incredible oatmeal raisin cookies in it. I picked up the bag and sprinted to the shed, ducking behind the far side of it, the only side where I was completely out of view of the house.

I opened the paper bag and reached for the first cookie. With the first bite, joy flooded through my body as I experienced true compassion and love in the form of a soft, sweet, chewy cookie. While many people erroneously equate food with love, at that moment, that cookie was the personification of that idea.

I'd like to say that I only ate one of the cookies at that point and saved the other three for later, but in the seeming blink of an eye, I had devoured all four cookies. It was as I was pulling the final cookie out of the bag, though, that I received my best gift of the day. There was a small piece of paper in the bottom of the bag. I pulled it out and read, "I thought you might enjoy these, Cool Papa." I had truly found the best friend I would ever have.

I moved to the front part of the shed when I was done eating the cookies and painted there while I waited, the cookies warm and loving in my stomach, the words on the note singing in my head. A short while later I heard a loud cough come from the road. I didn't turn to see Benjamin, but with my back to the road and my right hand busily painting the shed, my left hand, down at my side, gave a small wave. I had no idea whether he saw it or not.

As the week wore on, it became apparent that it would take me until at least the weekend to paint the entire shed, especially since it took me a long time to figure out how to paint the trim without making a mess of things. I was thankful that on Thursday afternoon Mom came and painted for a short while to help me out – she painted much more quickly than I did. I was mostly thankful, though, that she didn't come out in the morning, that Benjamin and I had had our chance to exchange our greetings, and that I had had the chance to privately gobble up the peanut butter-chocolate chip cookies he had left.

By Sunday morning I was nearing completion. I had covered the walls of the shed in red, gotten the ladder out so I could reach the top parts, and was working on the trim of the final window. Just before lunch time I put the final touches on that window trim and stepped back to survey the shed. I couldn't believe it – the shed looked fantastic. I walked around the building, taking it all in at one time. I couldn't believe what I had accomplished. Could I have done this? I made a second lap around the shed to inspect all the nooks and crevices – certainly I had to have missed something. There was no way it could look this good. But it did look that good. I hadn't missed a spot, not even way up at the top. I hadn't dribbled any of the white paint onto the red while painting the trim; the paint was spread evenly, neatly. It was immaculate.

As soon as the impact of what I'd accomplished sank in, I had one thought – tomorrow, Benjamin and I would finally play our baseball game.

I gathered up the brush, the remaining paint, the paint-smeared towels, and the other accoutrements of my work and carried them to the barn, put them neatly away, and dropped the paint brush into a glass of water to soak while I ate lunch – I'd dry out the brush later when all the paint had had a chance to rinse itself out of it.

I strode triumphantly to the house, suddenly ravenous, ready to show off the shed and my accomplishment to my parents.

Mom was fixing lunch when I entered through the screen door.

"How's it coming along?" she asked.

"I'm done," I said, more confidence and swagger in my voice than I'd ever heard before.

She smiled.

"That's wonderful, Jack. Let me put a little extra on your plate to celebrate."

I smiled too.

"John," Mom called out. "Lunch is ready."

As I sat down at the table, Dad entered the kitchen. He sat down across from me.

"I see in this morning's sports page," Dad said, "that the Fort Wayne Pistons have just announced their schedule for this winter. Maybe we should drive on up some time and see a game. What do you think?"

I wasn't much of a basketball fan, but it would be interesting to see pro basketball players in person and get a look at the big city.

"That sounds okay," I said.

"Just okay?" he said, a small grin on his lips.

"I'd like it a lot," I replied.

"Good."

Mom came over and put a plate of food in front of each of us.

"Jack has some exciting news," she said to Dad.

"Oh, yeah? What is it?"

"I finished painting the shed." I could feel my chest swell.

"Did you give it two coats?" Dad asked.

"What do you mean?" I could feel my chest shrinking.

"Did you go over the shed twice, giving it two coats of paint?"

"No," I answered.

"You're only halfway done then." He put his first bite of food in his mouth.

I was beyond devastated. It felt as if every ounce of blood in my body had suddenly run out of me, leaving me a lifeless, limp shadow of a human being.

"John, you haven't even looked at the shed yet," said Mom. "Maybe it doesn't need a second coat."

"It needs a second coat," Dad said. "I'm not gonna let the boy get in the habit of doing a half-assed job."

He put his head down and shoveled one bite of food after another into his mouth. I looked up at Mom, who stood behind him. Neither of us knew what to say, either to Dad or to each other. Eventually, Mom mouthed "I'm sorry" to me.

I sat at the table for maybe half a minute, staring at my plate as Dad filled his mouth with one bite after another. In the silence I could hear him give each mouthful three or four chews before swallowing. I felt sick to my stomach. Anger filled my soul. I got up from the table and headed for the screen door.

"Jack," Mom said, "where are you going?"

I kept walking.

"You haven't touched your food," she called out.

The screen door slammed loudly behind me as I stalked out of the house.

That week was my Trail of Tears. While certainly it was nowhere close to being as brutal and disgusting as the actual Trail of Tears, to a ten-year old it felt like a sentence of twenty years' hard labor. The only glimmers of light were my glimpses of Benjamin and the snacks he left me.

I was belligerent that week. Not in words – in fact, I didn't speak a single word to Dad for five days and barely spoke to Mom, my responses to her typically just a mumbled "Thanks" when she provided me with something to eat or drink. No, I was belligerent in how I comported myself when going to pick up the food Benjamin left for me. I'd see him drop the bag in the grass, give him a nod, and brazenly walk down the driveway to retrieve the gift, all but challenging Mom to see me, to question me about what I was doing. I'd walk back to the shed with the treats Benjamin left, keeping the bag in my right hand so my body blocked the view of it somewhat, but not worrying if the bag swung back and forth.

Part of me wanted Mom to find out. Part of me wanted her to question what was going on so I could tell her that Dad wasn't one-tenth the man Benjamin was. But I knew, even if she saw me and suspected that something she didn't care for was afoot, she wouldn't say anything. She was afraid of what she might find out, afraid of having to tell Dad what she knew.

Late that following Sunday afternoon, I finished with the second coat of paint. This time I didn't bother with taking a couple laps around the shed because I knew how good my work was. Dad was in the barn as I cleaned things up. We didn't speak as I put the brush in the cup of water and put away the few other things that were part of my labor for the last two weeks.

I walked up to the house, entering the empty kitchen through the screen door. I passed through the dining room on my way to the stairs and saw Mom sitting in the living room, sewing as she listened to the radio.

"Are you all done?" she asked hopefully.

"Yes, ma'am," I answered.

I mounted the stairs and went to my room, closing the door behind me. I stayed there the rest of the day and night.

As soon as Dad left for work the next morning, I emerged from my bedroom, filled with an excitement that had been smothered for more than two weeks. I barreled down the stairs.

"Where are you going?" Mom asked me from the living room where she was tidying up some magazines and newspapers.

"I'm going to the reservoir," I said, slowing down a little bit.

"Don't you want some breakfast?"

"No, thank you. I'm good."

Mom began to follow me as I moved through the dining room and into the kitchen.

"How are you supposed to play all day without any food in your stomach?

As much as I simply wanted to get going, I knew if I didn't eat something, or at least take something with me, I'd arouse suspicion.

"How about I take a cheese sandwich with me?" I suggested.

"You need more than that," Mom insisted.

"It's just that it's been two weeks since I've been to the reservoir. I'm really anxious to see if anything's changed."

She rolled her eyes.

"Okay," she said. "But don't come home two hours from now complaining about how hungry you are."

"Don't worry, I won't." I knew that two hours from then I'd be fat and happy – slightly tired from a nine-inning baseball game and my belly filled with plenty of Benjamin's wonderful food.

I ate a little bit of the simple cheese sandwich as I rode down to Benjamin's. As soon as I was sure I was out of Mom's sight, I tossed the rest of the sandwich onto the side of the road so a couple birds would have a fun and easy meal. A couple minutes later, I was at Benjamin's. I rode my bike around to the back of his house, jumped off it as I neared the door, and ran up to the door. I knocked furiously. A few seconds later, Benjamin appeared and opened the screen door.

"Well, if it isn't ol' Cool Papa himself," Benjamin said with a twinkle in his eye.

"Hi, Benjamin!" I almost screamed.

I threw my arms around his waist and gave him a huge hug. Benjamin hugged me back just as hard.

"You ready to play a little ball?" Benjamin asked after we broke our embrace.

"Am I ever!"

"You go on out and get the field ready. I'll be out in just a few minutes, ready to go."

"Okay," I said, rushing to get things ready.

We played catch for a little while to warm up. I told Benjamin all about what had happened, the words tumbling out of my mouth in a torrent of sentence fragments and incomplete thoughts because I kept jumping from angry thoughts about my father to confused musings regarding my mother to thankful praises for Benjamin's kindness. He listened patiently and intently to all I had to say, including to the vitriol I aimed toward Dad.

"Do you realize how much your father loves you?" Benjamin asked.

I had the ball and stopped mid throw to look at him in confusion.

"What?"

"While you might not agree with his methods, and while I might have gone about it in a different way, your father was trying to teach you something. It appears he succeeded."

"All I can tell that he succeeded in doing," I said, "is showing me how angry I could be with him."

Benjamin grinned.

"He did succeed in that as well," he said. "But he also taught you some other things."

"Like what?"

"Tell me again how you felt when you had finished that first coat of paint and saw what you had accomplished."

"I felt great." I threw the ball to Benjamin, and our game of catch resumed. "For five minutes, I was on top of the world."

"You felt proud of yourself for what you had accomplished because up to that point you had no idea you could do something so big, did you?"

"Yeah."

"I'm guessing your father knew you could handle the job, even when you didn't. For the rest of your life, you can look back on the time you painted that shed whenever you feel overwhelmed, any time you feel like the task before you is too much; knowing you were able to do such a great job on the shed will let you know you can handle the task before you, no matter what it might be. You have more strength and talent inside you than you realize."

I caught the throw from Benjamin and stood there for a moment. His words floated in, around, and through all my thoughts and beliefs that I had been clinging to for the last two weeks about Dad.

"He taught you something else," Benjamin said.

"What's that?"

"Patience," he said. "The man who has patience is the man who has everything."

I stared at Benjamin, noticing the same playful grin still on his face. I felt my lips form into a crescent that I couldn't fight to keep back.

"Who gets to bat first?" Benjamin asked.

Our game began.

As much fun as Benjamin and I had that day, the events of two days later would make me question what he said about my father loving me. I still question it to this day.

I had been at the reservoir all morning. I'd stopped by Benjamin's house on the way there to say hi, and he said he'd have some lunch waiting for me whenever I came back.

Around one o'clock, I had tired of exploring, swimming, and chasing frogs. I rode my bike back to Benjamin's. He was out on the front porch when I arrived, rocking and reading *The Catcher in the Rye*, one of the many, I thought at the time, crazy books he always seemed to be reading. I hopped off my bike, laid it down in the grass, and walked up to join him. He put the book down and smiled when he saw me. As I approached the porch, I could see a pitcher of lemonade, a couple glasses, and a plate with a sandwich on it waiting for me.

"You have a good swim?" Benjamin asked as I neared the porch.

"Yep. I had the place all to myself again."

"It doesn't get much better than that," he said.

"It sure doesn't."

I reached the porch, sat down, and quickly grabbed the sandwich off the plate and started eating. It was an apple butter and peanut butter sandwich, my favorite, the apple butter being hand made by Benjamin so it was nice and spicy. He poured lemonade into the empty glasses. I chewed quickly on a few mouthfuls, and spoke with a half-full mouth.

"I'm getting better with my backstroke. You'll have to come on down again sometime and see me do it."

"That sounds like an offer I can't refuse."

"What's that book about?" I asked.

"It's about a young man who's trying to figure out who he is and the world around him," Benjamin answered.

"Sounds boring," I said.

I plowed through a few more bites, which was all it took for me to finish off the sandwich, as Benjamin smiled.

"Thanks for the sandwich," I said. "It was really good."

"You're very welcome."

We rocked contentedly as I washed the sandwich down with lemonade. Benjamin sipped from his glass.

"You think I'll have any trouble making friends at school?" I asked.

"I don't see why you should," he answered. "A great guy like you – why, you'll need an appointment book to schedule in all the friends you'll have."

I smiled.

We rocked some more, content to watch the day go by.

"What's it like being black?" I asked.

"It just is," he said.

"Whaddaya mean?"

"If I asked you what it's like to have green eyes, what would you say?"

I thought for a long moment.

"I don't know," I said. "I don't even think about it."

"Exactly. It just is."

We both smiled.

For the next ten minutes we rocked, sipped our lemonades, and looked out over the corn fields. About that time we noticed, above the tall stalks of corn, a dust cloud rising up along the road, coming from the direction of my house.

"The traffic's gettin' crazy around here anymore," said Benjamin. "We'll need to get a stoplight put up soon."

"Yeah, right," I said, grinning.

The dust cloud drew nearer and nearer until finally the top of a pickup truck came into view above the stalks of corn. I stopped rocking and leaned forward.

"Uh, oh," I said.

"What is it?" Benjamin asked.

"I think that might be my dad's truck."

A few seconds later the truck emerged from behind the corn stalks at the edge of Benjamin's front yard. I saw Dad behind the wheel of the truck. I froze. Dad wasn't driving very fast as he went by. He looked right at me.

"Oh, no," I said.

Dad quickly hit the brakes. The truck came to a stop just past the driveway. He stared hard at me for a few seconds, craning his neck to look at me. His gaze shifted to Benjamin. I could see the fury building in my dad's eyes, even from that distance. Dad swung the truck around, driving a little bit up onto Benjamin's grass, and pulled to a stop in the road right in front of the house. He glared at the two of us for what seemed like an hour before calling out through the open passenger-side window in a measured, stern voice.

"Put your bike in the back and get in the truck, boy."

I hesitated and looked at Benjamin.

"It's all right, Jack," said Benjamin. "Do what your father says."

Slowly, I got up off the chair, made my way off the porch, got the bike, wheeled it to the truck, and lifted it into the bed of the truck. I looked back at Benjamin. For the first time since I'd met him, there wasn't joy on his face. I moved toward the front of the truck and got into the cab.

The short ride home was in complete silence. One time, I stole a tiny, sideways glance at Dad. Pure rage and hatred was on his face. I could tell it was building with each passing second.

He turned into the driveway, drove around to the back of the house, and stopped the truck. We sat for a long time – me frozen, Dad seething. A couple minutes later, he spoke.

"Get in the house."

I got out of the truck and walked up to the house, Dad following behind me, his footfalls crunching loudly on the gravel. We walked in through the screen door.

Mom was beginning preparations for that night's supper when we entered the kitchen. She immediately noticed the tension.

"What's wrong?" she asked.

"It looks like our son is a nigger lover."

I kept walking, my pace increasing slightly. I was nearly through the kitchen when I heard his voice.

"Boy."

I froze, my back to him.

"Look at me, boy."

I turned around. He walked up to me and stared hard down into my eyes. I stared right back, my chin raised high so I could look squarely at him, my body suddenly filling with resolve. Dad raised his hand and slapped me so hard across the face that I couldn't keep myself from dropping to the floor. Mom stared at us with her mouth hanging open.

"Get up," my father hissed.

I stood, my knees shaky, my resolve growing. He glared at me for a few long moments.

This time, when his hand came down toward me and slammed down across my ear, the concussion of the blow made my ear feel as if it had just exploded. I crumpled to the floor. The ringing in my ear made me shake.

"John!" my mother screamed.

"You stay there, Mary," said my father. "This is between me and the boy."

My father glared down at me.

"Get up," he said again.

I got up. I stared right into his putrid eyes. I was determined that if he hit me again I wouldn't go down. He raised his hand a third time, this time balled up into a fist. He savaged me across the face with that fist. I was no match for the blow – I collapsed to the floor.

As I lay there, my father hovered over me, his wrath far from spent. I didn't know what to expect next. Would he kick me? The thought ran through my mind that he might kick me in the mouth, and I'd go through the rest of my life missing half my teeth, the other kids forever making fun of me for looking like a hayseed. Or what if he kicked me in the eye and I was blinded by the kick? I'd never be able to hit a baseball well again. What if my life was never the same again because of the momentary anger exhibited by and acted upon by one dark-souled, complete imbecile?

He curled both his hands into fists that were poised to bludgeon. I looked over at my mother. Her face was filled with anguish, her body motionless.

"If I ever catch you with that nigger again," my father said as his fists opened and closed over and over again, "I will beat the livin' Hell outta ya. Go to your room. Ya better not come out until I tell ya to."

I rose. After a quick glance at him, I looked at my mother. We stared at each other. She seemed utterly weak and pathetic. I turned and went to my room.

I closed the door after I entered my bedroom and lay down on the bed. My head was on fire, my left ear roaring in my brain. I stared at the ceiling. For the longest time I wondered when the tears would come, but they never did. The long afternoon passed, the pain worsening with the quiet clicks and ticks of the clock that stood devotedly by me on the bed stand. I hoped Benjamin would be all right, that my father wouldn't take it into his pea-sized brain to seek retribution on a second innocent that day.

Daylight eventually faded to night. It wasn't until the moon had fully risen and had illuminated my room that the roar in my head subsided enough for me to close my eyes and find refuge in sleep.

Chapter Three

A shotgun blast ripped through the night and jerked me from my sleep. My eyes sprang open as I bolted upright, my heart pounding.

I took a moment to clear my head before rushing to the window and staring in the direction of Benjamin's house. Flames leapt high into the sky.

"Oh, god, no."

A pick-up truck roared by, the second of two that had just passed our house. By the stark moonlight, I could see the vehicle was loaded with men dressed in the white robes and hoods of the Ku Klux Klan. They hooted and hollered. Some of them fired off shotguns into the sky.

Terror flooded through me. I slid my overalls on, quietly slipped out my bedroom door, closed it behind me, and tiptoed down the stairs and out the back door.

As soon as I had gently closed the screen door, I broke into a sprint, my fifteen-year-old legs carrying me through the corn field, the cool soil moist around my bare feet, the leaves on the corn stalks slashing at my bare arms.

The whole time I ran, I could hear shotgun blasts ringing out and the Klansmen's screams rolling over the corn field. I ran as fast as I could, my lungs heaving from the strain, visions of a bloodied, fearful Benjamin – even a dead Benjamin – racing through my mind.

The shouts and gunfire grew steadily louder. Thin rivulets of blood formed on my arms, but I felt no pain, only fear.

My path became slightly more illuminated as I drew closer to the flames. I came to an abrupt stop as I reached the edge of the corn field. That's when I got my first good glimpse of the night's festivities. A few dozen Klansmen filled Benjamin's front yard. More were arriving as I watched. Pickup trucks filled the driveway and the front yard. A large cross burned in the yard.

Many of the Klansmen toted shotguns and periodically fired them into the air. Others trampled the flowers in the neatly attended beds; some were kicking almost comically at the plants because of their long robes getting in the way. A few of them yelled at Benjamin's house.

"You don't belong here, nigger!"

"If you know what's good for ya, nigger, you'll be outta town before the week's out."

The Klansmen whooped and hollered at the dark house. One of them threw a rock, missing the window that was his intended target. Another one hurled a rock of his own. This one shattered the living room window. Upon hearing the smashing of the glass, a whole group of them let out a whoop.

"Come on out, ya coon," shouted another Klansmen, "if ya think you're a real man!"

They continued to shout and shoot off their shotguns. The cross burned wickedly bright.

"Please don't set the house on fire," I said quietly. "Please don't set it on fire."

"Go back to the jungle where ya belong, you monkey!"

"Find somewhere else to live, spook!"

The Klansmen tore up flowers and trampled bushes. Some of them moved to the back yard and kicked over Benjamin's table and chairs while stomping through his garden.

A few went up onto the porch and knocked over the table and chairs there. One of them then moved to the front door and pounded on it.

"Come out, nigger!" he screamed. "Come out and take your medicine!"

The destruction, yelling, and gunshots continued for another ten minutes. The language grew more vulgar, the gunshots more frequent, but there were only so many things they could destroy. They began to lose some steam.

"Come on," one of them finally yelled out. "Let's get out of here before the cops show up!"

Dozens of the Klansmen howled and laughed at the thought. Mercifully, they made their way back to their pickup trucks, a few of them getting into the cabs of the vehicles but most of them piled into the beds.

"You're not welcome here, nigger!"

"Burn in hell, coon! You're lucky we didn't kill your black ass. Next time we will!"

The trucks peeled out, those that were parked in the yard tearing up the grass in huge chunks. A few more shotgun blasts ripped the night as they drove off. I could hear the shouts and screams trail off into the night as a few last epithets were hurled Benjamin's way. The cross continued to burn brightly.

As soon as I was sure that the last of the trucks was far enough away that I wouldn't be seen, I broke from between the stalks of corn where I had stayed hidden and rushed up to the front door, pounding hard on it.

"Benjamin! Benjamin! Are you okay?! Benjamin!"

A few seconds later the door opened to reveal a sleepy-looking Benjamin. He was in his pajamas and in a bit of a playful mood, a mischievous smile on his face.

"Did they wake you too?" he asked me.

"Are you all right?"

"I'm a little tired," Benjamin answered. "I haven't gotten much sleep tonight."

He smiled wide.

"Aren't you scared?" I asked. "Aren't you angry?"

"More sad than anything else," Benjamin said in a matter-of-fact tone.

"Sad?"

"Sad that so many people should be so afraid of one old black man that they should act like that."

"What?"

"Come on in and have a seat," he said. "Can I get you something to eat or drink?"

He turned and walked back into the house, flipping on some lights as he moved into the living room, stepping carefully around the chunks of broken glass. I followed him. His demeanor helped to settle me down.

"No, I'm good," I said.

"We'll have to get some salve on those cuts of yours." He looked at my arms.

"They're all right."

We sat down on a couple chairs, Addie and Jesse keeping an eye on us from a short distance away.

"How can you feel sadness about what just happened?" I asked.

Benjamin took a deep breath.

"Your dad has a gun in your house, doesn't he?"

"Yeah," I answered.

"Say you were sittin' out in the back yard one day and you saw an ant crawl by. Would you go in and get that gun and shoot it?"

"Of course not."

"Now say a rabid wolf came stormin' into the yard," said Benjamin. "Would you go in and get that gun and shoot that wolf?"

"Yeah. Who wouldn't?"

"Those men who were just here – they think I'm a rabid wolf who's a threat to their world," said Benjamin. "They don't realize that I'm just an ant, as insignificant as a speck of dust. They also don't realize that they're ants, too, and that the only way any of us ants are ever gonna make a bit of difference in this world is if we all work together."

"They still shouldn't've done what they did."

"No, but they did no real harm to me, only to themselves."

I gave Benjamin a quizzical look.

"Hatin' wastes so much energy," said Benjamin. "It only makes people angry and bitter. That's no way to go through life. Now, you wanna help me put that fire out?"

I smiled. "Sure."

We went out into the night and stared at the burning cross for a few seconds with its flames splashing against the darkness of the night.

"It's actually kinda pretty, glowing in the night like that," he said.

"Huh," I answered. "I guess it is."

It took us a while of throwing buckets of water onto the cross to extinguish it, but eventually the last breaths of smoke rose off the charred cross. We watched the tendrils of it drift off into the night.

"That wasn't so bad," said Benjamin. "We'll take it down in the mornin' when it's had a chance to cool off, and we'll get things cleaned up."

"Okay."

"You should get on home so your parents don't find you missin' and get upset," he said.

"All right," I replied.

I started to walk out to the road, deep in thought, the black of the night starting to engulf me as I moved farther from the glow of the house.

"Hey, Jack," Benjamin called out.

I stopped and looked back at him.

"Thank you," he said.

I nodded and resumed my walk.

It had turned into a beautiful night. There were no clouds in the sky. The moon was still bright. The stars were too numerous to count. I became aware that I was very sleepy. My thoughts turned to the Klansmen who had tried to destroy Benjamin's will. How many of them taught at my school? How many of them did I know? Were any of my schoolmates at Benjamin's house that night? How many people from church were there? How many of the Klan members were police officers or county sheriffs?

By the time I reached my house, I was physically and emotionally weary. I opened the screen door and stepped softly into the kitchen. I stood motionless and listened for any movement – there wasn't any. I flipped on a light, went to the cupboard, grabbed a glass, moved to the sink, and filled the glass with water. I turned, leaned back against the counter, and took a long drink of water. That's when I saw them – a few muddy boot prints and a dirty pair of boots on the floor by the door. I was sad and angry but not surprised.

I didn't say anything to Benjamin the next morning about my father. When I arrived at his house, he was already busy at work. In the daylight things looked so much worse. Years of cultivating plants and the yard and the nice things Benjamin had spread about for decoration were ruined. When I saw the destruction, I should have been filled with anger, but with him standing close by I didn't feel wrath or fury. All I could do was shake my head.

"For the thousandth time in my life," Benjamin said, "I've been taught that all things eventually pass." There wasn't even the tiniest hint of sadness in his voice. He was simply making a casual observation as most people do when they comment on a cloud drifting lazily across the sky.

Our first task of the day was to get the charred remains of the cross knocked down and moved out of the way. We both pushed on it. It immediately started to lurch. A couple seconds later it thudded to the ground.

"That wasn't too hard," I said. "They certainly didn't get it secured very well last night."

"It's difficult to do quality work when you're in a hurry," Benjamin said with a glint of playfulness in his eyes. "Now I'll have a little extra wood for the fireplace this winter."

"I guess that's one way to look at it," I said.

"Let's drag her on back behind the house and get her all chopped up."

"As you wish, Captain," I said. We smiled.

We both grabbed one of the arms of the cross and began to drag it around to the back of the house. When we went past one of his flower beds I surveyed the extensive carnage.

"I can't believe what they did to your flowers," I said.

"We might be able to save some of 'em."

We dragged the cross a little farther before Benjamin said, "This all coulda been a whole lot worse."

"How so?"

"They could've set the trees on fire. What would we have done for shade the rest of the summer?"

"Aren't you the laugh riot," I said.

Benjamin gave me a mischievous smile.

We worked through the morning, moving from one task to the next. The progress was slow but noticeable. My heart broke when I saw that many of the vegetables in his garden had been destroyed.

Around lunch time we made our way to the broken front window of the house. I held some plywood over the spot. Benjamin went along the edges of the plywood, hammering nails in to make the board tight to the window frame. Considering the events of the last twelve hours and my worries of the night before, a thought came to mind that I realized had never crossed my mind before. Being fifteen, I had to explore it immediately.

"Where are Addie and Jesse buried?" I asked.

"In a cemetery in town, right next to each other."

"Don't you ever go to see them?"

"No, I sure don't," he said.

"Why not?"

"Why should I go to the place where they're dead when they're still very much alive right here?"

I looked up. Benjamin stopped hammering, and we stared at each other. He had a clear-eyed, paternal look on his face. I was comforted.

Benjamin hammered a few more nails in.

"That'll do for now," he said. "I'll make arrangements to get it taken care of later this week."

"I can get into town this week with my mom when she does her shopping and get things taken care of for you if you want me to."

"You don't have to do that."

"I know I don't have to – I want to," I said.

Benjamin smiled.

"All right."

Benjamin hammered in another nail.

"That oughta hold her," I said. "Go make yourself comfortable out back. I'll bring you something cold to drink and a little something to eat."

"I can do that."

"Good. Now get goin'."

Benjamin grinned and scampered off.

As he went around the house, I went inside and made my way to the kitchen. I found the ever-present pitcher of lemonade in the refrigerator and poured out two glasses. I went back to the refrigerator, found a jar of Benjamin's homemade apple butter, and proceeded to make a couple apple butter and peanut butter sandwiches for us.

As I made the sandwiches by the sink, I looked out the window at him. He sat in a chair under the shade tree, smiling as if he didn't have a care in the world as he looked about the yard. He turned his attention to the corn field. Was he thinking about Addie and Jesse? Was he thinking about how he would fix up the yard now that he had a largely clean slate to work with? Was he remembering a time when he was younger, maybe a day when he lashed out a game-winning double in the bottom of the last inning?

Mechanically I made the sandwiches as I stared at him, the smile never leaving his face. What was it that was making him so happy? Certainly it wasn't the events of the night before. Then it hit me – Benjamin wasn't thinking about anything. He wasn't remembering events from his past or dreaming of the future, he simply was. He was breathing clean air, feeling the soft breeze on his cheeks, taking in the scent of growing corn. All he was doing was experiencing that moment, that magnificent, wonderful moment of fresh air and a gentle breeze, and he was gloriously happy.

Peace settled over me as I finished making the sandwiches. As I put them on a couple plates, cleaned up my mess, and set it all on a large serving tray, I noticed everything becoming more vivid. The mere act of cleaning up wasn't a mere act, it was somehow spiritual. My hand seemed to move gracefully and effortlessly across the countertop as I wiped up the bread crumbs. The simple act of putting the peanut butter back in the cupboard and the apple butter in the refrigerator seemed almost balletic. Something had changed, but I didn't know what. Maybe more importantly, I didn't really care what it was that had changed. All I knew was that Benjamin seemed to spend every minute of every day relating to the world in this manner. I hoped to have this for myself one day.

As I exited the back door, the sun was high overhead and warm. Benjamin sat on the chair, still happy and content. I carried the tray out to him and put it down on the small table we'd repaired not two hours earlier that was between us. I handed one of the glasses to Benjamin before I sat down.

"Thanks, Jack."

"You're welcome," I replied.

"I really appreciate all your help."

"Don't mention it."

We sat for a while and sipped our lemonades, the sandwiches waiting patiently between us. My mind wandered, the realizations of just a few minutes earlier slipping away.

"Has anything like this ever happened to you before?" I asked.

"Yeah."

"When?"

"Three or four years before you and your folks moved in, the boys paid me a visit. That time a bunch of 'em swore up and down that before the night was over a nigger'd be hangin' from a tree."

He grinned.

"They were wrong."

"Doesn't it feel kinda strange being the only black man in the area?" I asked.

"They're just adjectives."

"What adjectives?"

"Black and man," said Benjamin. "Strip away all the adjectives, and all you have left are people. I'm just one of thousands in this county."

"Doesn't it scare you sometimes, being the only black man around here? Especially when something like last night happens."

"When you're happy and have a good friend to share your days with, there's not much that can upset you."

"I guess you're right," I said.

"Haven't you learned yet, Jack – I'm always right."

He winked. We both sat back and enjoyed our lemonades.

As easy and comfortable as things were with Benjamin, the same couldn't be said for those times when I had to deal with my father. While Benjamin and I could sit and say nothing for long periods of time and both be completely at ease and content, when my father and I were alone together there was rarely much talking. The silence between us on those occasions was thick and heavy as I frequently wondered if I was just one slip of the tongue away from feeling his wrath.

Early that Sunday afternoon I found myself alone in the driveway with my father as we cleaned and gapped the pickup truck's sparkplugs. My father would unscrew a plug from the engine and hand it to me to clean and gap before putting it back in place. The words were few and far between as we worked, and they all had to do with the plugs and the truck, which largely bored me. I changed direction.

"How are things at the rail yard?" I asked.

"Fine."

I worked away on the sparkplug that was in my grease-smeared hands for a few moments while I waited to see if he would elaborate. He didn't.

"What all goes on there?"

"Ah, you know – trains come in, trains go out," my father replied.

He removed a plug he'd been working on unscrewing and handed it to me. I gave the cleaned and gapped plug to my father, turning to start on the plug that had just been handed to me.

"Did you hear all that noise the other night with the cross burning down the road?" I asked.

"Yeah, I heard some gun shots and all. It seemed like there was quite a ruckus goin' on down there."

"It was kinda loud," I said.

"It sure was."

We worked in silence for half a minute while I waited to see if a confession would come forth. It was naïve of me to think that way.

"Do you have any idea who any of the guys were who were down at that house?"

"No," said my father, "I don't think so."

We worked without talking for a while.

"Do you know what all ended up happening down there?" I eventually asked.

"Not really. Here ya go."

He handed me the sparkplug he'd just taken out of the engine. I handed the newly-cleaned and gapped plug back to him.

"So's your ma gotten ya your school supplies yet?" my father asked me.

"Not yet. She's gonna pick 'em up this week."

"Huh."

We worked without talking, the discomfort between us lingering. Though we had only been at this job together for twenty minutes or so, I was already beginning to feel emotionally drained.

"Ya know," he said, "I think I can handle things okay from here. Why don't you go on inside and see if your mother needs help with anything?"

"All right."

I put down the sparkplug I was working on and headed up to the house, thankful for the early parole for good, or maybe ambivalent, behavior. I went in the back door and entered the kitchen, where I found my mother preparing that day's lunch. I washed my hands in the sink.

"How are things going out there?" she asked.

"Okay, I guess."

"Are you already done with the sparkplugs?"

"No," I answered. "Dad said he'd finish up on his own."

"He doesn't need your help?"

"I guess not."

I dried my hands and looked in the refrigerator.

"Do you need help with anything?" I asked.

"You can set the table for me."

"All right."

I closed the refrigerator door and went about setting the table.

"What was going on with you in church this morning?" asked my mother.

"Whaddaya mean?"

"You sure looked like you didn't want to be there."

"I don't know," I said, thinking for a moment. "I guess I was just a little annoyed with the hypocrisy."

"What hypocrisy?"

"Well, among other things, it says in the Old Testament that we're not supposed to eat cloven-footed animals, but we had bacon for breakfast."

"A lot of things from the Old Testament changed when Jesus came along," she said.

"I imagine those things that changed were the ones that were the most convenient for us to change." There was more contempt in my voice than I had intended. I didn't look up, but I could feel her glare.

"What about a camel going through the eye of a needle?" I asked, my focus on the table. "That's New Testament. What about having compassion for prisoners and blessed are the meek and loving thy neighbor? We have one neighbor you and Dad hate. Those things were all taught by Jesus, but we just ignore all that stuff."

"Christians aren't perfect," she said.

"Shouldn't we at least be trying? It seems like most of us don't even make an attempt to live up to what the Bible teaches."

"The New Testament also teaches us not to judge others. It seems to me that maybe you're casting the first stone."

I continued to set the table in silence.

"These are good people around here, Jack. This is the kind of community you can be proud to be a part of. These people work hard. They're devoted to their families and their god. They have good morals – you should respect that."

"But what about…" I started to say.

"'Judge not, lest you be judged,'" she interjected. "When you finish up there, check the rolls in the oven for me."

"Yes, ma'am."

I silently continued with my work.

Over the next few days, things fell back into place amazingly fast at Benjamin's. In many ways, we both liked the changes that had taken place in his yard. He even managed to save some of the vegetables in his garden, which I noticed one day as we were having a leisurely game of catch in the back yard.

"Look at that zucchini you got comin' in," I said. "They're huge."

"We'll get some tasty bread out of 'em, that's for sure. Some of the apple butter will really taste good on it."

"Don't forget to…"

"Don't worry," Benjamin said, "I'll make sure I put plenty of raisins in each loaf."

I smiled. We tossed the ball back and forth a few times without saying anything.

"My father was one of the guys who burned the cross in your yard."

"Are you surprised by that?"

"I guess not," I answered. "It makes me angry, though. How could he be such a jerk? How can all these people around here be such idiots?"

"Don't let it bother you. People sometimes get caught up in things they really don't believe in because pretty much everyone wants to be part of a group. Look at the Nazis. Some really good people did some really disgusting things all because they were scared and wanted to be part of somethin' bigger, even if that somethin' bigger was doin' evil things. I'm sure many of those people are ashamed now of what they did and curse themselves every night as they fall asleep."

"Only because they lost."

"Maybe," Benjamin said.

By this time, I no longer threw my hardest to Benjamin since I could throw pretty hard and his reflexes had slowed a bit over the last couple years. Occasionally I spun a slow curveball to him for fun, but I had a sudden urge to really snap one off. I motioned to Benjamin with my glove that a curve was coming and threw a pretty decent one.

"That's comin' along nicely," he said.

"I'm a regular Bobby Shantz, aren't I?" I joked.

He grinned.

"Do you wanna be part of a group?" I asked Benjamin.

"Our nation of two is the only group I need to be in to be happy."

I smiled. We continued to toss the ball back and forth.

"Still," I said a moment later, "I'm sorry my dad did that to you."

"You don't have to apologize for someone else's actions. You do need to come inside and have some fresh oatmeal raisin cookies with me."

"I can do that."

"Good," he said.

He caught the last toss from me. We began to walk up to the house, Benjamin trailing behind me. I suddenly stopped.

"Hey – you be Vic Wertz," I said to Benjamin, "and I'll be Willie Mays."

"You got it."

I quickly got into an outfielder's fielding position.

"Whenever you're ready," I said.

"All right then. Here's the pitch…"

Benjamin wound up and, just as he released the ball, he made a simulated bat-hitting-ball sound as he launched a fly ball over my head. I raced back, doing my best imitation of the great Willie Mays in the 1954 World Series. I made an over-the-shoulder catch. I spun around and threw the ball back to Benjamin, the throw coming in to him almost right at his chest.

"Perfect!" he exclaimed. "You're a Hall of Famer if I ever saw one."

I beamed. The oatmeal raisin cookies tasted better than ever that day.

That night at dinner my parents were in an unusually happy mood as we sat around the table to eat. At least they were happy for a while.

"You sure we can't have some of that blueberry pie for dessert?" my father asked my mother.

"No," she replied. "I told you – it's for the church bake sale."

"Can't you just take some leftover mashed potatoes instead?"

"Nooo," teased my mother. "If you're not quiet, you'll get nothing but lima beans for dessert for the next two weeks."

"Oh, you're no fun," said my father, a rare grin on his face.

"How was work today?" she asked.

"Oh, it was somethin'."

"What happened?" my mother asked.

"We had a train from Detroit stop in on its way to Indianapolis. Me and the guys were workin' on it when this uppity nigger comes down out of the engine and starts tryin' to tell us how to do our jobs. That might play in Detroit, but that dog don't hunt here."

"What happened?"

"Let's just say that if the engineer hadn't stepped in, there'd be one less nigger in Indianapolis tonight."

"Could you not use that word?" I said.

"What word?" my father said in a mocking tone. "Indianapolis? Engineer?"

I glared at him. His mood quickly turned dark.

"First off, don't you ever tell me what I can and can't say, and what I can and can't do," my father said. "Second, you better not tell me you're still a nigger lover."

"Benjamin is more of a man than you'll ever be," I said.

His mood turned even darker.

"You say one more word like that and I'll knock every tooth out of that stupid skull of yours."

I looked back down at my food and fiddled with it.

"Thank you for proving my point," I said.

"Who put this food on the table?" my father asked, his voice rising. "Who put this roof over your head? Who's provided you every goddamn thing you have?"

"Except character," I said.

Like a flash, my father punched me hard in the face. I reeled a bit but managed to keep myself from falling off the chair. Out of the corner of my eye I saw my mother flinch, but she sat passively, afraid to intervene.

"You just tell me when you want some more of that," he said, "'cause there's a whole lot more where that came from. Get outta my sight before there's one less nigger lover sleepin' under this roof tonight."

I glared at my father, got up from the table, and left the kitchen. My parents remained silent as I walked out. When I had turned the corner, I heard my father say, "That boy's an embarrassment to the family."

I stopped, my head throbbing, waiting to hear my mother's response. Seconds that seemed like hours passed. She never said a thing.

I went up to my room, closed the door behind me, and lay down on my bed. For a long time I stared at the ceiling, feeling little but loathing and anger as my head continued to throb. I didn't shed a single tear.

The next morning I couldn't wait to get to Benjamin's house to experience the warmth and comfort of his compassion and love-filled home, to experience his kindness and caring attitude.

When I arrived, riding my bike around to the back of his house, I found him sitting in one of the chairs under the shade tree in the back yard. He had a plate of bread in his lap and was breaking it up into tiny pieces.

His face lit up when he saw me ride up the driveway, and my heart filled with joy. I got off the bike, laid the bike down in the grass, and walked toward Benjamin.

"Did you listen to KMOX last night?" he called out.

"No," I answered. "It wasn't the most conducive atmosphere last night for asking my non-baseball-loving father to tune in a game."

"You missed it then. Ol' Musial had three hits, including a home run." Benjamin shook his head in astonishment. "He's really somethin'. I sure would love to see that man play sometime."

I reached Benjamin and sat down next to him as he returned his focus to the bread.

"Why do you always break the bread up so small?" I asked.

"The birds have to work so hard for their food. I'm just tryin' to make it a little easier for 'em."

He looked up from the plate of bread and noticed the bruise on my face – the smile on his face quickly disappeared.

"What happened there, Jack?" he asked me.

"Dad and I had a disagreement."

"Are you all right?"

"Yeah," I said. "I'm a little sore, but all right."

"What was the disagreement about?"

I gave him a hopeless look. Benjamin responded with a small, knowing nod.

"I hate my father. He's an idiot, an embarrassment. I'm ashamed to be his son. My mom's no better. She never disagrees with him or tells him he's wrong or to shut up. She's a spineless woman."

"You shouldn't speak of your parents like that," he said. "It doesn't do anyone any good to speak poorly of another."

"But my father's disgusting."

"He's just scared. The world's changin' – it's always changin'. Most people fear change; we fear what we don't understand. Just look at Jackie Robinson and Larry Doby. They were just two men who liked to play baseball, and look at how people reacted to that. The people who hated them so much were just scared of how the world might be in another month or year or decade down the road. They didn't want their world to change."

"What if you'd been killed that night the Klansmen were here?" I asked.

"The flame doesn't seem to mind too much when the candle's blown out."

"I'd've minded."

Benjamin gave me a gentle smile.

"You know what my Addie would say about every one of those men from the Klan?"

"'If you took the time to look hard enough, to really get to know them, you'd find something beautiful and wonderful about them,'" I said.

Benjamin's smile grew wider. I had to grin a little myself.

We sat quietly for a short while as Benjamin continued to patiently break up the bread.

"When I was growing up, I thought my father was a god," I said. "He was aloof, a mystery, all-powerful. He seemed so massive and strong. I thought nothing bad could ever happen to me and my mom as long as he was around. Shortly before we moved here, he took me hunting. He told me the day before that we were gonna go the next morning. You wouldn't believe how excited I was – I'd never done anything so important, so grown up, with him before, or with anyone. That night I bet I only slept two or three hours. I kept thinking how thrilling and exciting it would be to be out in the forests with wild animals all around and tracking them with him. He would be like Daniel Boone, noticing almost imperceptible footprints on the ground as we tracked a great beast, seeing a small branch that was broken and somehow realizing the break was fresh, so an animal had been by just recently. He'd know what kind and how big an animal it was by the footprints and how deep they were, and by how high up the broken branch was. It wouldn't only be us doing the hunting. I pictured a wolf or a bear trailing us, looking for his opportunity to pounce on us, but my dad being fully aware of this the whole time, so without me even noticing, with me thinking that all he was doing was tracking an animal, at the same time he was completely aware of any animals that were hunting us, and he was artfully outmaneuvering them while staying hot on the trail of our prey.

"The next morning we were up by four-thirty and on the road fifteen minutes later. Dad didn't say a single word as we drove. Neither did I. I assumed silence in the truck was part of the hunting, part of the experience, that we were getting in tune with nature even as we rode in the truck. That made the silence between us exciting. We eventually pulled off the road by some woods and got out. Dad grabbed his gun out of the truck's bed, handed me a large paper bag, and told me to carry it. I did. I followed him into the woods. After maybe three or four minutes of walking, we stopped next to a tree. 'Here we are,' he said. I had no idea what he meant. He told me to climb up the tree. That's when I noticed there were wooden rungs hammered into the tree and a perch built into the saddle of a branch about ten feet up. I climbed up to the perch. He handed his gun and the paper bag up to me and climbed onto the perch, too. We sat there. For hour after hour, we just sat there in complete silence, waiting for a deer to come along. I was dumbfounded. No hunting, no tracking, no out maneuvering, just sitting, but I was afraid to say anything or to question what we were doing; the silence was no longer exciting. Every now and then Dad would break the silence as he pulled a can of beer from the paper bag and opened it. Eventually the quietness would occasionally be broken as he stood up and pissed over the edge of the perch every half hour or so. About five hours into this wonderful experience, he pulled a cheese sandwich out of the paper bag, tore it in half, gave me the slightly smaller part, and we ate it.

"Finally, about eight hours into this drudgery, a doe wandered right underneath our perch. It came from upwind, which was our only chance because I'm sure every deer for miles downwind of us could smell my dad's piss. This poor, stupid animal knew something wasn't quite right, 'cause she froze right underneath us, her nostrils moving, her eyes scanning about. She stood there so long my dad had more than enough time to slowly grab his gun through his semi-drunken state and aim it right at that doe. By the time he pulled the trigger, the barrel of that gun couldn't've been more than eight feet from that doe's head. Even in his half-drunken state he couldn't've missed that deer. Heck, a blind quadriplegic couldn't've missed that shot. When that doe dropped, why, you'd've thought my father had just single-handedly defeated the Mexicans at the Alamo with the way he carried on, yellin' and hollerin' and whoopin' it up like he was a big shot, like he'd accomplished something, bragging to me about what a great hunter he was. As I helped him drag that poor animal back to the truck, and as he kept bragging and carrying on like he was something special, I realized for the first time that he wasn't a god. He wasn't even close. I realized he wasn't even a man."

Benjamin had continued to break up the bread as I spoke, but now he stopped and looked at me.

"Don't judge your father too harshly. We can't know everything he's gone through, everything he's experienced, the things he was taught while he was growin' up. My guess is he's doin' the best he can, what he thinks is right."

"I guess," I said. "But it's still disappointing."

Benjamin grabbed a small handful of the bread crumbs and cast them out into the grass. As he was preparing to toss another handful out into the grass I asked, "What was your childhood like? Did you get along with your parents?"

"My childhood was somethin' special," Benjamin said with a smile. "I grew up in Chicago. I was fortunate to have two wonderful parents. They were both born as slaves in Alabama, which is maybe why they appreciated everything they had so much. They were so excited to have me teach them how to read. They were both illiterate when I was born. When I started school, every night after supper I'd get my grammar book out and go over the reading lessons from the day to teach Momma and Daddy how to read. By the time I finished the third grade, they could both read the newspaper each day. Boy, they were so proud of that."

Benjamin smiled at the memory.

"You know, one of the things I loved most about my childhood was the community. Everyone knew everyone else. I ate hardly a single supper as a kid where we didn't either have one of my friends sitting at the kitchen table with us or where I wasn't sitting at the table at one of my friends' houses and eating with their family. Back in those days everyone seemed to have a nickname,

including pretty much all of my friends – there was
Waddles and Topsy and Sweet Potato and First Pitch and
Wrinkle."

"'First Pitch'? How'd he get his name?" I asked.

"Oh, ol' First Pitch, every time we played ball, he'd
be so excited when he got to bat that no matter where the
first pitch to him was thrown, he'd swing at it, and
everyone knew he'd swing at it. First Pitch even knew he'd
swing at it. But he just couldn't help himself. Even if the
first pitch was a foot outside and at his ankles, he'd swing
at it. If he was lucky he'd miss the ball so he might get a
better pitch later in the at bat, but First Pitch was just a
good enough ballplayer that he could usually get the bat on
the ball, so he had a whole lot of first pitch ground outs
back to the pitcher and weak dribblers to second base and
little pop ups that were easily caught.

"But First Pitch wasn't the only kid in the
neighborhood with a baseball nickname. 'Wrinkle' was
also baseball related."

"What?" I said. "How could 'Wrinkle' be a baseball
nickname?"

"With Wrinkle, at about nine years old, he was still
just Toby. He decided he was going to start throwing a
curveball. He practiced throwing curves on his own,
throwing one after another against a brick wall in a lot
behind where he lived. Toby would come to school every
day and brag about these great curveballs he was throwing
at home. After about a month of practicing his curveball,
Toby was convinced he had developed this incredible
breaking ball. He gathered us all around one day to
demonstrate his new pitch.

"Toby sends Waddles down about fifty feet away
and tells him to get ready for the most incredible curveball
he's ever seen. The rest of us all gathered around. Well, he
throws his first curve. The ball spun a little bit, but it
couldn't have curved more than about half an inch. It was

terrible. Toby immediately started strutting around like a barnyard rooster, braggin' about what a great curveball he'd just thrown, and First Pitch said, 'That curveball there didn't break no more than a wrinkle – that wasn't a curveball, that was a wrinkleball.' From that day forward, Toby was known as Wrinkle. Boy, did he hate that name. But it fit 'im. For years Wrinkle pitched in our games, and his curveball never did get any better, but you couldn't tell him that. In fact, Wrinkle was so confident with his curveball that sometimes he'd announce from the mound that it was comin'. He'd stand there and call out to the batter, 'Here it comes. Here comes my nasty curve. Let's see if you can do anything with it.' The outfielders would immediately start backing up. I saw some of the longest outs any ten- and eleven-year olds ever hit at those moments. More often than not, the batter would rip into that measly little wrinkle of a curve that Wrinkle would throw, but we never had any fences, and whoever was playing left or center field would race back and catch the ball, and ol' Wrinkle would start struttin' around because he got the batter out, not even caring that the batter had just hit the ball farther and harder than any ten-year-old had a right to hit a ball."

"What was your nickname?" I asked Benjamin, a huge smile covering my face.

"'Hoss.'"

"What?" I said, my voice filled with incredulousness. "How could your name have been 'Hoss'?"

"It was Hoss because all through grade school, I was always the biggest kid in my class."

"You were?"

"I was," said Benjamin. "Those were glorious times. It was a lot of fun bein' the biggest kid around. I could hit the ball farther than all the other kids, and I could throw the ball harder. For years, I dominated our games. At thirteen, I was the same height I am today. At that point, I was growing at least three inches a year. I figured if I had one more year of three inches of growth, then a year of just two inches, followed by one or two more years of a mere one inch of growth, I'd end up six-foot-four, or maybe even six-five. Alas, I stalled out at five-ten. But I'm kind of glad it worked out that way because I got to experience baseball from the perspective of being the big slugger everyone looked up to and who struck out two out of every three batters who came to the plate because I could simply overpower them with my fastball, and I got to experience baseball from the perspective of being a line-drive hitter who had to use his speed to make things happen on the field and who had to develop a whole arsenal of off-speed pitches to get batters out on those occasions when I did pitch.

"My friends and I didn't just play baseball, though. We were always runnin' around the neighborhood and in and out of each other's houses. Momma would be in the kitchen cleaning up the dishes from breakfast, and I'd rush by her, fly out the back door and call out, 'I'm goin' out to play.' Sometimes, I wouldn't be home again until it was dark out. My buddies and I would play Kick the Can and Fox 'n' Hounds and Ox in the Ditch and Hide-n-Go-Seek and all kinds of games all day long – we didn't have a care in the world. It seemed like our whole lives revolved around which game we were playin' or which game we'd play next. We'd even play Cowboys and Indians. Can you imagine that sight – a bunch of young Negro boys runnin' around pretendin' they were cowboys and Indians, whoopin' it up like crazy men? Boy, we had some fun." Benjamin's smile seemed to stretch from one ear to the other.

"Did you ever get in any trouble?" I asked.

"Nah, I never did anything to get in trouble. At nine, I started smokin', though. Boy, did I think I was a big shot. I'd stand around in front of my friends like I was somethin' special, like I was the king of the world as I puffed on a cigarette. After two weeks of this, it occurred to me that the money I had spent on cigarettes was enough to have bought a delicious dinner for Momma, Daddy, and me. I thought to myself, 'I'm takin' food out of my parents' mouths.' As much fun as my childhood was, it was also often a struggle for my daddy to keep us fed. I stopped smokin' right there, and I've never smoked another cigarette since."

"Did you get good grades in school?"

"They were okay. I coulda worked harder, but my teachers always liked me," he said with a grin.

"Were you a slacker in school?" I asked teasingly.

"I like to think I was a daydreamer," he said. "For instance, one time when I was eleven years old, I happened to come across a newspaper article about King Kelly and whether he should be considered alongside Cap Anson as maybe the greatest baseball player in Chicago history. They had a picture of Kelly in the paper with his big, bushy mustache, and they told tales of his shenanigans on the field and how he could hit the ball maybe as hard as anyone had ever hit a ball and how he had invented the hook slide. For the next two weeks at school, I don't think I heard more than a dozen words my teacher said. I'd just sit at my desk all day long and stare out the window and daydream about what it would be like to be King Kelly and play all those games all over the country in front of all those thousands of people and have a big, bushy mustache like he had. I bet half a dozen times a day during those two weeks Miss Williams said to me, 'Benjamin, would you care to join us?' The other kids would giggle. For maybe a minute and a half, I'd try my best to pay attention to her lesson. Before I knew it, I was back to daydreamin' about ol' King Kelly and his baseball exploits."

"I wish I had a childhood like you did," I said. "I'm jealous."

"Don't be," he replied. "We all have our journeys to travel."

An image from the night before of my father punching me flashed through my mind. I shook my head.

"Maybe, but I'd sure like to change a thing or two about my journey," I said quietly.

"One thing I've learned over my many years," said Benjamin, a little twinkle in his eyes, "is that there are two things that can always chase my worries and disappointments away – a nap and some warm apple cobbler with ice cream on top. Since it's too early for anyone to be takin' a nap, we're gonna have ta settle for the apple cobbler I just pulled outta the oven not ten minutes before you arrived. Okay?"

A smile slowly appeared on my face.

"Okay," I said.

"Come on."

We got up and headed for the house – Benjamin spread the rest of the bread crumbs in the grass as we walked.

I sat down at the kitchen table when we entered the house, and Benjamin went to work. The cobbler was still warm when he spooned the ice cream onto it. By the time he placed the food in front of me, the ice cream was starting to melt. It was all I could do to wait sixty seconds longer until the ice cream got even softer and he had joined me before I dug in. With the first bite, I was in heaven.

"Oh, my," I said with a full mouth. I closed my eyes to fully experience the bliss.

"There aren't many things better than cobbler and ice cream in the morning." said Benjamin as he put the first bite into his mouth. "Mm mm," he moaned.

For the next few minutes we ate in rapturous, blissful silence, the quiet occasionally broken up with a moan of ecstasy from one or the other of us.

We finished our plates at the same time. Benjamin gave me a mischievous look.

"You up for another go 'round?" he asked.

"Oh, yeah," I answered.

"I was hopin' you'd say that." He grabbed our plates, went back to the counter, and loaded them up again.

Five minutes later we were sitting, fat and happy, in the living room, with me wondering if life could get any better. It could.

"Hey," Benjamin said. "Do you know how to drive yet?"

"No," I answered. "My father said he would teach me this summer, but he hasn't gotten around to it."

"Well how 'bout we make today the day you learn how to drive?"

I felt my eyes get huge.

"Really?" I said. "Can we start now?"

"Absolutely," he said. "Let's go."

I scrambled out of my chair and rushed to the back door.

"Come on," I called out as Benjamin trailed behind.

"Don't you worry. I'm hurryin'," he said.

I ran across the yard and to the barn, feeling as if I was in a fantasy land where breakfast cobbler with ice cream and morning driving lessons were the norm. Before he was even half way across the yard, I had the barn doors open to reveal the old Woodie. It had never looked more beautiful. I rushed to the door on the driver's side.

"Not so fast, Jack," Benjamin called out. "I'll pull it out of the barn and demonstrate a few things for you before you get to drive."

"Aw," was all I could say.

For the next ten minutes, Benjamin drove slowly up and down the road, talking me through everything he was doing, making sure his instructions about shifting gears were easy to understand. The last couple minutes of his demonstration I barely heard a word he said as I frantically rocked back and forth on the passenger side, my impatience the equal of a seven-year-old's on Christmas morning.

Benjamin pulled the car to the side of the road.

"Do you think you're ready?" he asked me.

"Yeah, yeah, yeah." I nodded my head. I was so giddy I may have been salivating at that time like a dog with a steak dangling in front of him, but I don't know.

Benjamin turned off the ignition and got out as I slid across the seat. A moment later, he got in on the passenger side.

"All right," he said. "Make sure you push in on the clutch when you're startin' her up."

I did as instructed, turned the key, and the Woodie roared to life.

"Woo-hoo!" I shouted.

"All right," Benjamin said. "Put her in first gear and slowly press down on the accelerator as you slowly let out on the clutch."

Again, I did as instructed, but my timing was a little off. The Woodie took off like a bolt of lightning, spewing gravel behind us. Our heads snapped back. The engine whined, straining as I quickly hit twenty-five miles per hour while still in first gear.

"Press in on the clutch," Benjamin shouted with joy. "Let off the accelerator so you can shift into second!"

Methodically, I managed to execute his instructions. After a brief pause to make sure the transmission was in second gear, my lead foot had the Woodie once again screaming down the road. I looked over at Benjamin. We both cackled like hyenas.

I ended up driving around rural Huntington County for nearly an hour that day. By the time we returned to Benjamin's house, even though I had stalled the Woodie on multiple occasions during the first fifteen minutes of our drive, I felt like an old pro, smoothly shifting from one gear to another, and even learning how to come to a complete stop simply by downshifting without ever touching the brakes. I felt like a grown up as I turned into his driveway, drove around back to the barn, and backed the Woodie into the barn as smoothly as could be done. We got out and walked to the front of the car.

"That was mighty impressive," Benjamin said.

I knew what to say, but as I looked at him, I couldn't get my mouth to open or my tongue to work. After a couple seconds, I simply stepped forward and threw my arms around him, hugging him with all my strength. He did the same. Eventually, I was able to get out a muffled, "Thank you."

"You're welcome, Jack," Benjamin whispered. "You're welcome."

That Saturday morning I was in my room reading a beat-up copy of *Player Piano* by Kurt Vonnegut that a schoolmate had given me on the last day of classes in June. I had been reading it on and off during the summer. I had really started to get into it, feeling myself travelling to a different world every time I picked it up. I was more than two-thirds of the way through the book and was already dreading its conclusion, wanting the story to go on and on with no end.

I was completely immersed in the book when I heard my mother call from downstairs.

"Jack, can you come on down here?"

I finished the paragraph I was reading, placed my bookmark, and hurried down the stairs.

"Yeah, Ma, what is it?" I asked as I stood before her.

"I need to get these towels up on the line to dry. Can you go to the garden and pick some peas for lunch?"

"Sure." I went to a cabinet, found a bowl, and headed for the screen door, holding it open for my mother as she went out before me with a laundry basket full of wet towels.

"Where's Dad?" I asked as we walked along.

"He left early this morning to go hunting with some guys from work."

"Huh," was all I answered.

As my mother made her way to the clothesline, I veered off for the vegetable patch. Our garden was especially lush that summer with plenty of peas, okra, tomatoes, squash, zucchini, pumpkins, and watermelons. I began to harvest some peas when the okra really caught my eye. It was perfect – big enough to be plump and juicy, but not so big as to be tough and stringy. I grabbed one and took a bite out of it. Utter happiness flooded through me. I took another bite and finished it off.

Before I knew it, four or five minutes had passed with me doing nothing but standing there and eating one okra after another. I was as lost in a world of okra as I had been fifteen minutes earlier with the world of *Player Piano*. The entire universe had been reduced to me and a single okra plant.

"Jack!"

The yelling of my name snapped me out of my happiness. I looked up to see my mother, still over by the clothesline, staring at me, an annoyed look on her face.

"What are you doing?" she asked.

"I'm eating some okra," I answered. "It's wonderful."

"Stop it," my mother said. "You're not some animal that sneaks into a garden and eats up all the vegetables. Fill that bowl up with peas."

"Yes, ma'am."

I went back to picking peas, the luscious flavor of the okra lingering in my mouth, a trace of the joy I had just been experiencing still present.

Chapter Four

As usual, that November my parents and I spent Thanksgiving Day together. Mom had done her usual fantastic job of preparing the house and the meal for the day. Everything was as perfect as it could be. As nice as it was, I was mostly looking forward to sneaking away after the meal when Dad fell asleep to go see Benjamin.

My father and I sat in strained silence in the dining room. The table was already covered with enough food to make a dozen people happy, but my mother had one more thing to add to the menagerie. She had gone out to the kitchen to get it. As I sat next to my father I wished she had two more things to bring in so I could have gone with her to bring in the last of the food.

"Things good at school?" he asked.

"They're fine," I answered.

"That's good."

Silence returned.

Finally, my mother turned the corner. She carried a casserole dish to the table, using oven mitts to protect her hands, and she placed the dish on a pad she had waiting for it on the table.

"That's everything," she announced.

"It sure smells good," my father said.

After she placed the oven mitts on the hutch next to the table, my mother sat down with us.

"Everything certainly looks great," my father said.

"Thank you," my mother replied. "Will you say the prayer, John?"

My father nodded.

"Let's bow our heads," he said.

My mother and father closed their eyes and bowed their heads. I bowed my head a tiny bit but didn't close my eyes. I watched them as my father prayed.

"Lord, we thank you for all you have blessed us with – for this food, this house, this family. We thank you for sendin' your son, Jesus, to die on the cross for us so that we may live forever. Thank you for watchin' over us and protectin' us, for keepin' us, your children, safe in your love…"

I glared at him out of the corners of my eyes.

"…and for every blessin' and gift you bestow on us daily. In your heavenly name we pray. Amen."

"Amen," said my mother.

My parents opened their eyes and looked up. Mom gave a big smile.

"Let's eat," she said.

They dug in. I put quite a bit on my plate – Mom's twice-baked potatoes were always rapturous – but I made sure not to eat too much. Benjamin would have a tableful of even better food down at his house. I wanted to make sure I had plenty of room in my stomach for his tasty treats.

My father and I had assumed nearly identical eating styles by this point in time, shoveling food into our mouths in a continuous manner so that we wouldn't be expected to say anything. Speaking with a mouth full of food was inconsiderate in my mother's eyes. She was slightly more delicate in her manner and occasionally started up a little conversation during meals. Dad and I had become quite adept at making sure we were relegated to primarily grunts and nods during meals.

Two hours later, after plenty of eating, Mom and I had cleaned up most of the mess in the dining room and kitchen, and she and Dad were both napping. I quietly slipped out the back door and headed down to Benjamin's. When I entered his house I was overwhelmed with the smell – the scents of a dozen incredible dishes mingled into one head-spinningly wonderful scent.

"Hey, Benjamin." I took off my jacket and tossed it over the back of a chair.

"I'm in the kitchen, Jack."

I headed for the kitchen and found Benjamin cooking away. The foods he had were amazing. My mother could make some tasty dishes, but she was nothing compared to him. Even though I wasn't particularly hungry after eating just two hours earlier, I felt my mouth moisten. My gaze fixed on his sweet potatoes and the pecan pie he'd made. I knew that utter bliss would soon be mine.

"How'd things go with your parents?" Benjamin asked.

"Pretty well," I answered. "The food was good, and the conversation was light. Dad even smiled a couple times."

"That's great. Hey," Benjamin said, "can you try a bite of the scalloped potatoes to make sure they're okay and still warm?"

"Are you kidding? Of course!"

His scalloped potatoes were served on Mt. Olympus – they were a food reserved for the gods. He knew how much I loved them.

I grabbed a spoon and shoveled a heaping mound into my mouth. My knees became weak. Through a full mouth I mumbled, "They're great."

Benjamin smiled and winked.

I finished chewing and swallowing.

"Can I start taking things to the table?" I asked.

"Sure," said Benjamin. "I'd appreciate that."

Fifteen minutes later we were seated at the dining room table and eating like it was the first time we'd ever seen food. We talked and laughed through mouths filled with food and expressed our incredulity that the Dodgers and Giants were leaving New York.

"How can there not be baseball in Brooklyn?" Benjamin asked, his eyes wide. "I think it's a sign of the apocalypse."

"I can't believe Willie Mays will no longer be playing in the Polo Grounds," I said. "If anyone was ever made to cover all that ground, it was Willie."

We passed food back and forth to each other. I must have moaned out loud a dozen times, the meal was so wonderful. I couldn't imagine any place on the planet being more perfect than sitting at Benjamin's dining room table with him across from me on Thanksgiving Day. A small part of me felt sad knowing that the chances were slim I'd ever experience something so wonderful again, but I quickly banished that thought from the forefront of my mind and simply immersed myself in the happiness of the moment, of being surrounded by my favorite foods and sharing those foods with my favorite person.

We ate and ate. Just when I thought I couldn't get another bite in my mouth, Benjamin said, "You ready for some pecan pie?"

As full as I was, I nodded excitedly.

We took our pecan pie into the living room, made ourselves comfortable in the chairs, and enjoyed every bite of the pie, even the crust. When I'd swallowed the final bite, I placed the small plate on the coffee table in front of me, then sat back.

"That was the greatest meal of my life," I said. "Thanks so much, Benjamin."

"I'm glad you enjoyed it."

He finished off his last bite, put his plate down, and looked at me. From the gleam in his eyes, I knew he had something up his sleeve.

"What is it?" I asked.

"I went somewhere Monday," Benjamin said.

"Was it anywhere fun?" I asked.

"I went into town and met with a lawyer," he said. "I had a will drawn up." He paused for a moment. "I'm leaving everything I have to you, Jack."

"What? Why?"

"Because you're every bit as much my son as Jesse is. You should inherit this house and my possessions."

"Don't you have any family you can leave your things to?" I asked.

"I have some distant cousins in Chicago," Benjamin said. "But I haven't seen or heard from any of them in years and years – heck, I don't even know for sure if they're still alive. Why should they get my house and car and money? You should get it."

"Are you sick?"

"No," said Benjamin, "I feel great. But at my age, you never know what might happen."

I sat there, not knowing what to say.

"Don't worry," he said, a smile returning to his face. "You're not going to be a millionaire when I die. The house is paid for, the car is paid for, everything in the house is paid for, and I have a few dollars in the bank."

"Thank you, Benjamin," I finally said.

"I love you, Jack. You make my life special."

I looked at him and wondered how I'd been so lucky to know a man like him.

On the first day back to school after Thanksgiving break, my art teacher gave us an assignment – we had to paint a picture. It had to be completed by Christmas break. Her only instruction regarding the content of the painting was that we had to paint something beautiful. Within fifteen seconds, I knew exactly what I was going to do. I knew I would give the painting to Benjamin for a Christmas present.

I immediately went to work. I got my canvas, some paint, and some brushes, and got painting. I was no Picasso or Pollock, but I had become rather proficient over the years in my art classes, and I had decent painting skills.

By the end of that first period of working on the painting, the outline was rounding into form. The painting was a high-angle view of Benjamin's back yard the first day we ever played catch together. I could see every detail of that day so clearly, even more than five years later. I could see the flowers growing around the yard, the pumpkins getting big in the garden, the shade tree standing watch over us, the Woodie peeking out of the barn. All of these things were either already making their first appearance on my canvas or they soon would be.

Before the school day was over, I had become obsessed with my painting. I couldn't quite explain why I was so fixated on it, but at least part of it was because I'd never been able to come up with a great gift for Benjamin for any of his birthdays or Christmases since we'd known each other. All the gifts I had given him over the years were silly trinkets I'd found and could afford from Woolworth's. He always said he loved the gifts. His smile was always radiant when I'd give him something. My heart was certainly in the right place with each of the gifts I gave him, but I knew deep down they were lousy gifts, especially the tiny, gray stuffed mouse I got him for his birthday four years earlier. What had I been thinking in getting him that gift? I could no longer remember my rationale for believing he'd like it. I saw this painting as my first chance to give him something really special.

The next morning I had trouble focusing in both geometry and U.S. history as I awaited third period and my chance to resume work on the painting. When I did finally get to art class, I poured myself into the work. I had to get every detail right and make sure I didn't forget a single item, no matter how insignificant it seemed, down to the small potted daffodils he had in front of the barn for a short time before he replanted them in the ground on the side of the house later that summer when they'd grown bigger.

Before I knew it, nearly all of my free time was spent contemplating how I could make the painting as good as possible. Was I talented enough to include more than the most basic shadows cast by the tree and the barn? Was there a fine enough brush in the room for me to include a few zucchini on the ground in the garden? It was torture being able to work on the painting for only forty-five minutes a day, five days a week. Day after day, I was the last student in class to leave the room, putting off cleaning up my area until the last possible moment to squeeze in a few more brush strokes or finish off one more flower before having to go to biology.

The weekends were the worst. A few times I even contemplated – not seriously – breaking into the school to have four or five quiet hours where I could focus on the painting and really make some headway on it. I was able to pull myself away from those thoughts by recalling Benjamin's maxim – the man who has patience is the man who has everything.

The days flew by as it seemed I might not have enough time to finish the painting by Christmas break. I had my moments where I doubted the painting was any good, but two or three times a week Mrs. Rohling would stand over my shoulder and watch me paint for ten or fifteen seconds and tell me how good it looked before she moved on.

There was one detail I had to save for last. It had to be the absolute final thing I added to the painting – Benjamin. On the last day of class before Christmas break I would take a spot in the corner of the room where no one could see my painting and add him in then. I would make sure to be the last student to leave class that day, and I would bring a towel with me to cover the painting when I walked down the halls with it at the end of the day.

When I added him into the painting, he looked as perfect as I hoped he would. Since it was a high-angle view of his yard and of me and him playing catch, I didn't have to paint any details of his face. Facial details were a particular weakness of my painting skills. Not only was Benjamin perfect, so was just about everything else, right down to the gloves on our hands and the ball flying through the air, me in my follow through and him preparing to catch it. I couldn't wait to give Benjamin his gift.

The last day of school before Christmas break started was Friday the twentieth. That Tuesday, Christmas Eve, after my father left for work, my mother and I decorated the house for Christmas. When I was a child, my parents had always waited until after I had gone to bed on Christmas Eve to do this. They would put up the tree, decorate it and the house, and wrap the presents, all in the hours while I slept. When I'd awake on Christmas morning, usually around four-thirty, I'd be convinced that Santa had worked a miracle while I slept – he was just like Superman or Jesus, or maybe a combination of the two. My parents would arise with me, functioning on just an hour or two of sleep (of which I was completely oblivious) and begin the day's festivities. They really did do their best to make sure I had lifelong memories. Many times over the years, when I was convinced my father hated me, I'd think about the lengths he went to make Christmases special for me. I'd realize that as frustrated and angry as he might be with me at the time, deep down there was a part of him that really loved me.

My mother and I were in the living room hanging some garland when she said, "Are you looking forward to going to Churubusco tomorrow and seeing everyone?"

"I suppose so," I said without much enthusiasm.

"What? You don't want to spend Christmas Day with your family? Uncle Bob and Aunt Sadie will be there."

"It's not that," I said, "I just wish they could come here."

"It's a whole lot easier for me, you, and your father to go there than it is for the twenty of them to come here."

"I know."

She pulled a small box out of a large cardboard box and handed ornaments to me.

"Can you decorate the hutch with these?" she asked.

"Sure."

I took the box to the hutch and set it down. I pulled out ornaments one by one and situated them in various places on the hutch as she continued with the garland. We didn't talk as we worked. When I finished, I turned to her.

"Does Dad like me?" I asked.

"Your father loves you," she answered quickly.

"I know he loves me – he's my father, he pretty much has to. But does he like me?"

Mom was silent for a long moment, her mind working. She finally spoke.

"You and your father are just going through a rough stretch right now. That happens sometimes when a young man like yourself is going through adolescence, especially with two very strong-willed people like you and your father are. You and he are actually quite similar in many ways."

My stomach retched at that thought. I didn't know what to say.

"Don't worry," she said, "this'll all pass. One day I bet you'll find your father's not too bad of a guy, that you actually like him."

"Maybe," I said.

She smiled a little as she took a large wreath out of a box and held it up.

"Come on over here and help me with this wreath," she said. "Where do you think we should hang it?"

"Over the toilet?"

Mom was playfully taken aback.

"Jack," she admonished, a smile on her face.

She really was pretty when she smiled. I smiled a little myself.

"No?" I said. "Okay, we'll put it on the front door."

I took the wreath from her. We walked together to the front door, my mother rubbing my back as we went.

That afternoon she took a box of decorations up to her and my father's bedroom to add a little Christmas spirit there. I saw this as my chance. I hustled to my room and went to my closet. There I found the painting I'd made for Benjamin, still covered in the towel I'd used to conceal it with when I brought it home. As I heard Mom humming "Jingle Bells" and fussing about in her bedroom, I tucked the painting under my arm and tiptoed down the stairs, trying to sneak out without being noticed. As I reached the bottom of the stairs I heard footsteps. As Mom came into view, I tucked the painting around the corner and out of her sight.

"You need something to eat?" she asked from the top of the stairs.

"No," I answered, "I thought I'd go for a little walk and get some fresh air."

She looked at me for a moment and gave me a knowing nod.

"Just make sure you're home in time for supper," she said.

"Thanks, Ma," I said.

I put my jacket on and nearly ran to Benjamin's house with the painting. The only thing that kept me from breaking into an all-out sprint was the fear that I might drop it.

When I reached his place I slowly opened the front door and peeked in. He was nowhere to be seen. I stepped into the house. Benjamin had a few tasteful decorations spread around the living room and dining room. The house smelled wonderful. I turned toward the kitchen, where I could hear him making a little noise.

"Something smells great," I said as I slid the painting behind a chair and took my coat off. Benjamin called out from the kitchen.

"Come on in here and have yourself some pie."

I went to the kitchen. Two fantastic-looking pies were on the stove. My eyes grew big.

"Wow," I said.

"Have yourself a seat there," said Benjamin. "Get ready to taste the best rhubarb pie you ever got your mouth on."

"Better than last year's?"

"It's so much better than last year's, once you put a bite in your mouth you'll say to yourself, 'I may as well die right now, 'cause it ain't ever gonna get any better than this.'"

I smiled and took a seat as Benjamin placed a large slice of pie and a glass of milk in front of me.

"When you get done with that," Benjamin said, "I'll get you a nice slice of boysenberry."

I took a bite and rolled my eyes in ecstasy.

"Oh," I said. "This is the best pie in the history of mankind. How do you do it?"

Benjamin smiled.

"You know how I do it."

"You've certainly taught me how you do it, but my pies never taste as good as yours."

I started watching Benjamin make pies when I was eleven, the two of us chatting away as he rolled out dough and prepared the filling. Eventually I became interested in what he was doing and noticed the different spices he added and techniques he used. By the time I was thirteen, I would ask him questions about how he made the pies. By the time I was fourteen, I was helping him make the pies. We had reached the point where sometimes I did the baking while he sat and watched me as we chatted away. While I knew my pies tasted good, they weren't yet Benjamin-good.

"Don't worry," he said. "Eventually they will."

I kept eating.

"So how're things goin' with your folks?" Benjamin asked. "Everything okay?"

"Yeah, everything's fine. My dad and I just kinda stay out of each other's way as much as possible. About the only time we really see each other is at supper. Ma's gotten pretty good at steering us all towards civil conversation."

I shook my head.

"Dad doesn't know anything about anything," I said. "He doesn't know anything about books or science or baseball or anything. All he ever wants to talk about is work. He's so boring."

"Just make sure you don't give up on your father," Benjamin replied. "He's the only father you'll ever have. One day you may find out he's not so bad after all. He probably knows a thing or two about topics you know little or nothing about. Someday down the road, when you get a bit older, you may even end up likin' him a little bit."

"You sound like my mother," I said.

He chuckled.

"I guess if the Dodgers can win a World Series, then anything's possible," I said.

Benjamin grinned. I laughed, took another bite of pie, chewed a few times, and moaned with delight. "I wish I could be here tomorrow instead of in Churubusco."

"Don't worry, you will be," said Benjamin.

I took another bite of the rhubarb pie and moaned again. I looked up. "I have something for you. Come with me."

I rushed to the living room. A smiling Benjamin followed. I pulled the painting out from behind the chair.

"Merry Christmas," I said.

He held the painting up in front of himself and stared at it.

"I made it in art class," I said.

Benjamin stared at the painting for a long time and gently ran his fingers over it.

"This is wonderful," he finally said. "It's exquisite."

"It's of the first day we ever played catch," I said.

Benjamin continued to stare at the painting. He finally looked at me. His eyes were moist. He put the painting down and took me in his arms.

"Thank you, Jack."

Benjamin hugged me as I wished my father would but never had.

The embrace ended. He looked down at the painting for another moment. A smile came to his face.

"Come on," he said. "I know right where I'm gonna hang it."

Benjamin picked up the painting, quickly walked toward the stairs, and went up them. I followed him and realized I had never seen the upstairs of his house before. It was so peculiar to think that there was something about Benjamin I didn't know. He went straight to his bedroom with me close behind him, my head swiveling around to take in as many of the new sights as possible.

As we entered his bedroom my gaze went straight to the only wall decoration in the room: an old, framed print of van Gogh's *Starry Night* hanging over the head of the bed. Benjamin moved directly to the print. When he reached it, he turned and handed me my painting.

"Here," he said. "Hold this."

He took the print off the wall and set it aside.

"I like yours better," he said.

I handed Benjamin my painting. He utilized the thin wire I had attached to the back and hung it on the exposed nail. Benjamin stepped back and looked at it.

"That's as perfect as it could possibly be," he said.

He turned and looked at me.

"I have something for you. You wait here. I'll be back in a minute."

Benjamin walked out of the bedroom and to the other end of the hallway. He disappeared around a corner as he entered another room. I looked around his bedroom. It was simple, almost Spartan. On the dresser was every single one of the presents I had given him over the years: the Satchel Paige baseball card, the handmade birthday card I gave him the first year we knew each other that had a simple tree and a smiling sun on it with "Happy Birthday" scrawled across the front in big letters, a set of jacks we had played with a few times, and even the little gray stuffed animal mouse. I couldn't believe it – my presents had meant something to him. They had meant a lot to him.

I was snapped out of my reverie when I heard his footsteps moving back toward me along the hardwood floor. I kept my back to him for a couple seconds as I fought back a tear. As he drew near, I turned around to see he was carrying a large cardboard box.

"Merry Christmas," Benjamin said.

I said nothing as he handed the box to me, afraid that should I open my mouth an embarrassing sob would sneak out. I took the box to the bed, sat down, and pulled back the flaps on the top of the box. My eyes widened.

"Oh, my gosh," I exclaimed.

I pulled the item out of the box to get a good look at it. It was a hand-carved wooden eagle; its wings outstretched – a full two feet from wing tip to wing tip – a single rose in its talons. It was astonishing. I placed the eagle in my lap and caressed the wings, the body, the rose.

"It's the most amazing thing I've ever seen," I said softly.

I stared at the eagle for what must have been close to a minute as I continued to run my hands over it before looking up at Benjamin.

"How long did it take you to make this?"

Benjamin smiled gently and shrugged.

"This is the best gift I've ever received," I said.

"As was mine," said Benjamin. "Come on. Let's go back downstairs so you can finish your pie."

I smiled and walked out of the bedroom with the eagle, Benjamin following behind me. I had never felt so loved in my life.

I had a good Christmas Day. My mother, my father, and I woke up early and opened our presents before driving to Churubusco. A gentle snow fell during the journey. The Indiana countryside looked beautiful. Uncle Bob made me laugh with a whole handful of new tales of his adventures and shenanigans, including telling me all about his recent trip to Las Vegas, which I'm sure he embellished quite a bit (but I didn't care). There was plenty of great food, but all day long I continued to think of Benjamin, alone in his house. I wished I could have been with him.

Winter turned bleak as we moved into January. The days were cold and mostly dark as a bank of clouds settled over us and didn't seem to move for weeks. One night when I couldn't sleep I got out of bed and looked out my window. The crescent moon broke free from the clouds for maybe half a minute before disappearing again. I realized, even with the long winter nights, it had been at least three weeks since the clouds had parted long enough for me to catch the merest glimpse of the moon.

One afternoon in mid-January I returned home from school to find my mother in the kitchen busy chopping some potatoes.

"How was school?" she asked as I placed my books on the table.

"Fine," I answered. "I'll be back in a little while."

"Okay, but don't be too long. I want you home before dark."

"All right." I went back out into the cold.

I hadn't seen much of Benjamin the last couple weeks as I was busy taking care of some end-of-semester projects that would soon be due. I walked briskly down the road, partly due to the cold weather and a desire to get out of it as quickly as possible, and also from a yearning to see my friend.

I reached his house and entered through the front door. I took my coat and gloves off.

"Hey, Benjamin," I called out, the house smelling of freshly-baked cookies.

I put my coat and gloves on a chair and headed to the kitchen. As I walked through the living room, I took a peek at the framed photos of Addie and Jesse and couldn't help but smile when I saw for the thousandth time that there were now a couple small school pictures of me tucked into the frames of the two photos. A moment later I reached the kitchen.

"Benjamin?"

I scanned the kitchen and saw that it and the adjoining bathroom were both empty. There was a plate of chocolate chip cookies on the counter, which was fairly normal. There were dirty dishes in the sink, which was very much unlike Benjamin. He always cleaned up behind himself as he went along.

I walked around the main floor, checking the dining room and looking about, but he was nowhere to be seen. The house seemed oddly quiet.

I went back to the kitchen and looked out the window toward the barn. The barn door was closed, and there were no tire tracks in the snow. Benjamin hadn't taken the Woodie out.

I went upstairs. I hoped Benjamin hadn't gotten sick and had to put himself to bed, that he had merely felt a bit tired and decided to take a nap before cleaning up the kitchen. He was taking more and longer naps recently.

I softly called out "Benjamin?" as I mounted the steps.

I reached the top of the stairs and slowly walked toward the open door of his bedroom. I reached the doorway and stopped. I stood and stared for a long time, frozen to the spot.

On the bed he lay, unmoving, his eyes open. He was hugging my painting tight in his arms. I continued to stare at the motionless Benjamin.

Slowly, I began to walk toward him, my steps short and soft. When I finally reached him, I stood over him. Benjamin looked serene, content. I shifted my gaze to his chest and stared down at it, hoping to see it move under the painting.

It didn't.

Benjamin's body was still warm and moved easily as I removed the painting from his arms. I put the painting aside, resting it on the floor against the bedpost. I raised his head and slid onto the bed, resting his head in my lap. I looked down at him, still hoping I might see his eyes blink or his lips part wide enough for him to take a breath, but neither of those things were going to happen. A few moments later I raised his head and cradled it to my chest.

The corners of my mouth trembled. My eyes filled with tears as I held Benjamin tight. I stared out the window at the approaching darkness and waited for evening to come.

Chapter Five

It's been nearly six decades now since Benjamin died. I'm an old man, the same age he was when he passed.

I still live in his house. Though I've lived here for more than half a century, it's still Benjamin's house.

My parents wanted me to sell off the house right away. There was no way I was going to do that. There was no way I could have done that. My parents and I had quite a few arguments over whether to sell the house or not, but I finally found the rationale that convinced my parents that I shouldn't sell it: There was no way we would get market value for the house since pretty much everyone within twenty miles of us knew that a black man had lived there. Not only would few people be interested in buying the house at any price, those who might be interested in purchasing it would certainly have only paid maybe half what it was worth.

Just like Benjamin, and just like my father, I spent my life working for the railroad. The summer following Benjamin's death my father got me a job at the rail yard. He said it would toughen me up and that I needed to have my own money for the upkeep of Benjamin's house. There was no way he would let any of his money go towards it. By the time I was in my mid-twenties, I was an engineer. Over the years I saw nearly every one of the forty-eight continental states. I met wonderful people just about everywhere I went, but I never stopped calling Huntington home.

My father and I forged a decent relationship over the years, but it was never what could be described as close. He remained a bigot to his dying day (he could barely contain his joy when he'd heard that Martin Luther

King, Jr., had been assassinated). It was impossible for me to be particularly close with someone I didn't respect. I was closer with my mother, but even that relationship wasn't particularly close or loving. I could never shake the feeling that, to a certain extent, my parents were strangers to me.

I never threw out any of Benjamin's things. I always had the sense that if his things were still in the house, he was still alive in some way. I did box up most of it. Some of it I moved into closets, some of it to the attic, some out to the barn. The photos of Addie and Jesse are still in the living room. I found a framed photo of Benjamin buried in a box in an upstairs closet and put it with the photos of Addie and Jesse, so the little family is all together again. The baseball gloves, ball, and bat that he and I played with still have their special place in the kitchen where we always left them between games of catch and the nine-inning one-on-one games we'd play. The painting of me and Benjamin playing catch in the back yard still hangs over the bed. Every time I look at the painting I'm still ten years old, and he's still alive.

The Woodie still has its home out in the barn. While I can't say it's in cherry condition, it still looks good. My Jessica and I take it out six or eight times a year for a drive. For the entire drive we laugh and carry on like a couple teenagers. There's something almost magical about that car, as if it's a time machine, and I really get a kick out of the thought that I still have the car I learned to drive in.

I also still have the same rocking chairs on the front porch and lawn chairs in the back yard that Benjamin and I spent so many hours sitting in. My Jessica often joins me in sitting in the chairs. While we sit in them, we talk and laugh and drink lemonade and eat pie and talk about how I finally got to see the Cubs win a World Series. Sometimes we sit on the rocking chairs on the front porch late in the day, saying little, and simply watch evening sneak its way in over the cornfields.

My Jessica is something special. What Addie was to Benjamin, my Jessica is to me. She's been the most incredible wife and friend I can imagine (and, boy, is she pretty). She's crazy about the squirrels around here. She's always tossing bread and peanuts to them, and she's given at least a dozen of them names. How she can tell one of them apart from another I have no idea. Every day I'm thankful that she chose to cast her lot with me.

I've never gone to Benjamin's grave site other than for his funeral. He was buried next to Addie and Jesse. My mother was the only other person who attended the funeral, besides a preacher who delivered a brief, perfunctory service. She showed not the least bit of emotion. When I began to cry, she did nothing – no arm around my shoulders, no comforting words. I've never gone back to visit the gravesite because why should I go to the place where Benjamin is dead when he's still alive where I live?

I ended up becoming a decent ballplayer. My senior year of high school I was playing catch after school one day with one of my buddies who played for the Rogers Friendly Markets semi-pro team in Huntington. Rogers Markets played games all over northeast Indiana, and sometimes went to Indianapolis, northwest Ohio, and even southern Michigan to play. My buddy noticed that I had a good arm, and I could run pretty fast. He got me a tryout with the team.

The manager was really impressed with my fielding and throwing and running, but since I didn't have a whole lot of experience batting off live pitching other than against Benjamin and the kids at school during recess, he said I could practice with the team that summer and work on my hitting. He couldn't promise me I'd get in a game, or even dress for a game. I didn't care, I was simply ecstatic to be on my first baseball team.

The last two weekends of the summer, though, I did get to dress for our games. It was such a thrill to put on a baseball uniform and sit on the bench with my teammates for the first time. I even got into two games, playing the last inning of both of those games in center field. I didn't get any at bats, but I was so excited about having played in my first real games that I spent that fall and winter not-so-patiently waiting for the next season to begin.

I never became a great player during my five years with the Rogers Friendly Markets team, but my hitting improved enough that by my third year with Rogers I was the starting centerfielder. I could run down fly balls in the gaps and rob hitters of what they were sure was going to be a double or triple. My arm was strong enough that every summer I'd gun down a handful of base runners who tried to go from first to third on me or score from second on a single.

I had one shining moment as a ballplayer. As long as I live, I'll never forget that day. My fourth year with Rogers Markets we had a really good team that qualified for the state tournament. We lost our first game to drop into the losers' bracket of the double-elimination tournament, but we won our next two games. In our fourth game, we went to the bottom of the ninth inning trailing 2-1. There were two outs and a runner on first when I came up. The pitcher threw me a curveball that came in a little high. I ripped the ball out into left-center field. As I sprinted down to first base, I saw the leftfielder and the centerfielder collide and the ball go by them to the fence. As I was approaching second base, the centerfielder was still lying on the ground while the leftfielder was staggering to his feet. I had a chance for an inside-the-park home run that would win the game.

As I tore around second base my hat flew off my head, and then something strange and wonderful happened.

I've never been one to believe in ghosts and the supernatural and other such things, but at that moment when my hat flew off, I felt, without any shadow of a doubt, Benjamin fill my body. Just as surely as I'm breathing as I write this, Benjamin and I suddenly became a single entity as I flew around second base. I could feel the exhilaration flowing through his body and the pure joy in his heart. At that moment, we were absolutely and unquestionably one.

As I approached third base, I could see the coach frantically waving me around third and on to home. Behind him, I could see my teammates in the dugout jumping up and down and waving me home as well. In my heart, my brain, my soul, my entire being, I could feel Benjamin bursting with joy and happiness and pride as we churned around third and ran as fast as we could.

I crossed home plate with the winning run. My teammates mobbed me. Over the next thirty seconds or so, I felt myself drowning in elation even as I felt Benjamin slipping away. I wasn't sad – I was completely thrilled to have experienced him so fully and completely one last time.

We came up short the next afternoon in the losers' bracket final to finish third in the state. It was a great season, memorable for so many reasons.

The older I get, the more I realize that Benjamin was right with just about everything he ever told me, including the fact that I would one day get the knack for making great pies like he did. In fact, I became so good at baking pies that I became a bit of a legend in Huntington County for my skills. It's due to the fact that I won the Huntington County Fair pie baking contest nine years in a row, every year baking a different pie that Benjamin had taught me how to make – rhubarb, apple, boysenberry, pecan, peach, sweet potato, raisin, sugar cream, and even the often dastardly mince. I still had a few more pies I could have broken out for the fair – my personal favorite is the blueberry pie – but I'd had my time in the sun. It was time to allow someone else to take home the blue ribbon.

The only thing I can think of that Benjamin told me that wasn't true was that if you simmered anything long enough and with enough sugar, you could make a pie out of it. As hard as I try, I haven't yet been able to come up with a dandelion pie that I would serve to others.

I still make at least one pie a week. I always feel closest to Benjamin when I'm baking something he taught me how to make. Most of the time when I think of him, a broad smile floods over my face, or sometimes I even laugh out loud. My Jessica, when she sees one of these silly grins on my face or hears me suddenly laugh at seemingly nothing, will always happily say, "Are you thinking about Benjamin again?"

Once or twice year, though, I think of Benjamin and don't smile or laugh. Sometimes I'll be baking a pie, or maybe I'll be in the spare bedroom where many of his clothes still hang in the closet, and I'll catch the scent of him. I suddenly start crying in violent, shoulder-shaking sobs that rip me to the core. They feel as if someone is reaching into my chest and ripping my soul right out of me. I've lost a lot of things in my life – both of my parents have died, my Jessica had three miscarriages, many of my friends have passed – but the only loss I've never gotten over is Benjamin. All these decades after his death it still feels as if it occurred just yesterday. He was the greatest teacher I ever had, the greatest person I've ever known. I'm still devastated that he's no longer around.

I love you, Benjamin. I miss you every day of my life.

The End

About Glenn Berggoetz

Glenn Berggoetz is the author of seven books and the writer of twelve produced feature films. These films have won numerous accolades with *To Die is Hard* being selected as the 16th-best B-movie in cinema history in the *Paste* magazine ranking of the 100 greatest B movies of all time, with two other of his films selected as one of the ten best independent films of the year by various critics. *Waiting for Evening to Come* is Glenn's second novel.

Social Media

Twitter – https://twitter.com/GlennBerggoetz

Facebook – https://www.facebook.com/glenn.berggoetz
https://www.facebook.com/glennsbooks/

Acknowledgements

I need to thank Alan Greene and Edward Done for their feedback on early versions of this work. Their insights added depth to the material and kept me going.

Thanks need to be extended to filmmaker Meryem Ersoz for her support of the project as it was in its screenplay format. I've long appreciated her belief in the script.

I want to thank my mother, Rosemary Berggoetz Arnett, and my brother Paul Berggoetz for their feedback on the material when it was in its infancy. Their thoughts let me know I was on the right path.

I need to thank Melissa Miller at Solstice Publishing for not only bringing *Waiting for Evening to Come* to the public, but for taking a chance on my first novel, *Two Loves*. I'm incredibly appreciative of her for giving me a chance.

Many thank yous to editor K.C. Sprayberry at Solstice Publishing. Editing work is an arduous process, and she has been a real go-getter throughout the process.

Finally, I want to thank the agents for actors Samuel L. Jackson and Albert Hall. These agents expressed to me their interest in having their clients possibly play the role of Benjamin should the screenplay version of the book be put into production, and this belief let me know that the material in this project resonates.

If you enjoyed this story, check out this other Solstice Publishing book by Glenn Berggoetz:

Two Loves

Jack Connelly has spent a decade toiling in the minor leagues. His long-time girlfriend Amy wants him to quit the game he loves and take a job with her company. But when Jack suffers a freak injury, he's suddenly a better ballplayer than he's ever been before, and with a chance to go to the major leagues, Amy makes Jack choose between her and baseball. Jack reluctantly chooses baseball and wonders if he'll ever love again. When Jack makes it to the major leagues, though, he soon finds himself falling hard for Laura, who just might be the girl of his dreams. Thoughts of Amy, however, still linger, leaving Jack to have to make the toughest decision of his life.

https://www.amazon.com/Two-Loves-Glenn-Berggoetz-ebook/dp/B00872AWTW/

Made in the USA
Monee, IL
25 January 2020